Love,
Life's Eternal Flame

Love, Life's Eternal Flame

Belle Chisholm

Love, Life's Eternal Flame

Copyright © 2021 by Vera B. Akomah. All rights reserved.

No part of this publication may be reproduced, stored in a retrieval system or transmitted in any way by any means, electronic, mechanical, photocopy, recording or otherwise without the prior permission of the author except as provided by USA copyright law.

The opinions expressed by the author are not necessarily those of URLink Print and Media.

1603 Capitol Ave., Suite 310 Cheyenne, Wyoming USA 82001
1-888-980-6523 | admin@urlinkpublishing.com

URLink Print and Media is committed to excellence in the publishing industry.

Book design copyright © 2021 by URLink Print and Media. All rights reserved.

Published in the United States of America

Library of Congress Control Number: 2021913425
ISBN 978-1-64753-870-5 (Paperback)
ISBN 978-1-64753-871-2 (Digital)

11.06.21

"Dedicated to Q-Tip, my companion, my little Alpha Dog"

DEDICATION

"Love is Life's Eternal Flame"

He then strikes a match as to light a fire and said, "Val, when you love, really love that someone or something for that matter, it's like life's eternal flame that burns deep in your heart, eternally. That love is a flame that never goes out.

CHAPTER

One

As I laid back in the chaise on the Patio with Diego and Asia lying on the cool patio surface, I thought back over the previous year, DJ now back at his unit in Afghanistan. My thoughts drift back to the tragic loss of Q-tip. My heart is so empty without his presence.

It's been a long hard six months. I can't help thinking it was all my fault. I keep hearing Daniel saying, "Val, you're beginning to sound like me. Just like you said it was not my fault what happened to DJ. It's not your fault what happened to Q-Tip."

I just wish I could really believe that in my heart. It still hurts so much when I think of him. I was so sick with grief for weeks. I could not get out the bed. I did not know how to get over his death. He was my heart, my comfort and my friend I could confide in when I had no one to talk to. I still ache when I think of him and when I walk in a room expecting to see him.

I truly know now, how some people feel when they have lost that someone who means the world to them. I finally really know how Daniel felt when he lost his son. I can never question how Daniel felt when he lost DJ. I know why he has so much interest in DJ's life. I laid back to rest my eye. The crew made a soft growl as Daniel tipped through the house. He leaned over and kissed the top of my head. I asked, "How was your trip?

"Much the same as always" "So how is Janelle doing with her treatments?" "She's coming along, according to her specialist, but it has a lot to do with her frame of mind. Her doctor said, it's not unusual for her to act in this manner. It's mainly because she's mad, at herself because she can only blame herself for not taking care of herself. Prognosis are great if she only stop rebelling against what the doctors and the staff are trying to do for her.

Honey, it's been less than a year since she's been there. I know she has made a big change since the day we took her there. Her analysts said she has come a long way since then, but she still has a long way to go. She still blames me and others for why she has cancer. When I'm there I spend as much time as I can with her, but I'm afraid she may get the wrong idea about my visits.

She tends to want to talk about when we were together and how much we were in love but, I don't like to indulge her in that conversation, because it only leads to arguments and she tends to get aggressive and bring up other things from the past. When she gets like that I usually tell her I have to leave or I'll miss my flight time. It's never a pleasant visit when I'm there. She's been diagnosed Bipolar as well.

I asked, "Does she get many visitors?" "Not to my knowledge, last time Danielle was there they had a big falling out and she told her not to come back again. Let her die in peace. So Danielle hasn't been there since. That was over three months ago." "Oh, Daniel that is so sad" "I know Val, but Janelle brings a lot of this on herself. She keeps that up she will get what she asks for, to die in peace, alone" "Daniel, that's mean." "I know Val, but there's only so much you can do for someone who doesn't want anyone's help. She told me she didn't want my pity or help.

This is what she told me when we first took her up there. Janelle doesn't want people to help her. She just wants to mistreat people, because it was what she liked, mistreating people who cared about her. She came from a very strange family. Her parents were never married and she was a much abused child. She was raised by her grandmother who gave her anything she wanted. She mistreated her because she could get away with it. I used to tell her don't treat her like that.

She used to say she ain't my mama. She used to curse Miss Hattie out so bad and had the nerve to say, she's sorry afterward. When Miss Hattie got sick, that's when she got pregnant. She had no one to turn to but me. Unfortunately for me, I was really in love with her. Miss Hattie died and left her the house and we lived there for a while.

She sold the house and went shopping, brought all this stuff we couldn't afford and we were about to have twins. That's when she told me she got pregnant so she could get on welfare. I told her my kids were not going to be on any welfare. So I told her let's get marry.

Like I told you, I was in college and doing pretty good. I was somewhat of a good student. After the twins were born we got married. I quite school and went to work. I joined the National Guard and realized I had to do something about my family.

All through our first years of marriage all Janelle talked about was if she hadn't got married, she would be on welfare and her kids would be taken care of. I had enough of that, so I made a big decision to enlist in the AGR program. After that you know the rest of the story.

Val, for years I tried to understand why Janelle was the way she was. She was never happy. No one could ever do enough to please her or make her happy. Lord knows I tried. I finally realized Janelle was a person who did not like herself. So, she made others dislike her because of how she felt about herself. She didn't care about anyone but herself. I saw that in the way she treated Miss Hattie.

She was the only person who loved her more than I did, at that time. She treated her so badly and didn't even want to go to her funeral, until I made her. Miss Hattie loved her, and she never would show just a little love for her. I never could understand that.

I finally realized Janelle hated her grandmother, because Miss Hattie was not her mother. She lived in that house with Miss Hattie and Janelle's mother until her mother decided to leave. When her mother left, she did just that, she left. She left Janelle with her mother. A bitter child who took it out on her grandmother every chance she got."

I then said, "Now look at her she may even die as a bitter old woman". "You right, that may be what she wants." "Daniel that's a sad story, I have to give you credit, you are a good person. You have a heart of gold. After all you been through with Janelle, you still stand by her side."

"Val, she's the mother of my children and there is no way, I can let her spend maybe these last days alive and not feel I owe her something. I plan to be there for her until that time. I hope you understand that?" "I do."

He then asked, "What's our plan for dinner." "I was hoping you had some." "What you want to do? We could go out to dinner since Soup's on vacation" "When is Soup coming back? I miss his company and I'm sure the crew does too." "I hope soon, when he gets down in the "Big Easy" with his friends and relatives, he forgets all about us." "Well, it's too quiet when he gone." "Well, why don't we go out for dinner?"

CHAPTER Two

We went and changed and went out to dinner. When we got back the lights were on in the back of the house and the kitchen. Daniel said, "I thought we cut the lights out before we left." "I thought so, too." Daniel then said, "Stay in the car" as he reached for the weapon in the glove compartment. "Daniel, be careful" I warned. Daniel was gone a good minute.

I then decided to see what was taking him so long. As I walked round to the patio and peeped through the gate. Daniel turned and said, "Look who decided to sneak home for a visit." DJ and Trinity were sitting at the patio table eating, with Asia and Diego. They both got up and came over and gave me a big hug and kiss.

I asked, "What you two doing here in the middle of the night?" "Nana we just wanted to surprise you and come see the most important people in my lives"

I looked at both of them and said, "So, what's going on between you two? DJ, you usually call and let us know when you coming in." "I asked the same question," Daniel invaded.

As we sat at the table, DJ then looked at us both and said, "Pops, Nana; Trinity and I are both Staff Sergeants now and since everything is winding down as far as conflicts going on.

We've decide to get married. I've asked Trinity to marry me. We decided to come here first and ask for y'all blessings." Daniel raised his eyebrows and very calmly Daniel asked, "What bought this all about, now hear me out son.

I know you are almost twenty four years old and you are a grown man. So, is there some particular reason you both want to do this, now? After all you both have very promising careers going." I echoed, "Um hum."

DJ offered, "We have talked on various occasions about marriage. Well, since we got promoted we've both been selected for recruiting duty. So, in order for us to continue to be together we've decided to get married and continue our careers together. When we get married, this is the one duty assignment the Army will not separate us because of our duty.

Nana you know how recruiting duty works." "Yea, it has its advantages and disadvantages for married couples. I had quite a few friends who were married and on recruiting duty together.

Are you sure there isn't any other reason why you want to get married now?" "No, Nana. Trinity is not pregnant. I know how your intuition works."

"I just wanted to know. Recruiting duty is fun, but it's hard on married couples. It can hurt some of the most devoted couples, and it has caused a lot of divorces for that matter. Take my advice as one who spent almost ten years in recruiting. I've seen some of my closest friend's relationship shattered because of applicants and mission pressure on each or both individuals.

The worse is that it's even harder on the individuals if you are not married or if one is not in the Army. All I have to say, if this is what you both want, you need to be each other's support channel through this whole tour. You are going to need each other's support. Knowing you two, you're going to be alright.

So, that's enough about recruiting duty. I turned and looked at Daniel, "So what you think, honey?" He smiled, and gave that old familiar wink and said, "Y'all have our blessing, and son thanks for making us a part of your decision and plan.

Now, that we got this all straight, Trinity have you talked to your parents, yet?" She said, "No sir, not yet." DJ intervened and said,

"That's where we're headed next. Like I said, we wanted to know how y'all felt first." "So son, what are you on leave?" Daniel asked. "No, we took a three day pass to come down here after our unit got back from deployment.

We both got promoted while on deployment and when we got back a few days ago we had orders for recruiting command. We talked about our plan and I mentioned since Nana had been a recruiter for about ten years we should see what she thought about our plan. I knew if anyone would tell the truth about recruiting she would." I smiled and said, "And I love you too." I then asked, "So when's the big day?"

"We haven't decided yet. We been looking at rings and we haven't decided on that yet either. It's just that things seem to be in a fast forward mode now."

Daniel casually advised, "You know it's getting late and I think we all need to turn in. Trinity, let's get you in the guest room." DJ interrupted, "I put her in Mom's old room if you don't mind." I looked at Daniel and said, "No, not at all." Daniel added, "You know the rules." "Yeah pops, I know the rules.

If you got a moment I need to ask you something." "Sure son." Trinity and I got up and walked towards the kitchen. She said, "Val, I am a little tired, I think I'm going to turn in for the night." "Ok, honey. I see you in the morning, good night." I then walked in the family room and poured me a glass of wine." I sat in front of the fireplace and sipped my wine.

Daniel walked in and said, "I was just about to do the same before turning in. You're doing one of my things." "What's that?" Drinking your wine and looking at the fireplace with nothing in it." "Oh, I was, was I? So, what you think?" He came over and sat beside me and asked, "About what?" "Ooh, about a marriage and our DJ wanting to get married."

He took my hand in his and said, "Honey, that young man has not been our DJ for almost three years, ever since he met and fell in love with that young lady.

He's so much in love with that young lady he wants to make her so happy. He told me, he's so in love with her, he's afraid he can't make her as happy as he see you and me. I told him don't just make her happy.

Happiness can be a temporary thing. The best advice I can give you is make her a part of your life and you must be willing to be a part of her life. You two are making the first step, by committing yourself to each other careers. That was the downfall in your grandmother Janelle's and our marriage among other things.

He said he likes the way we have our little private discussions and make decisions from those discussions. He wants to have, what we have. I told him having that type of relationship takes work. Its believing that one person in the relationship does not always have the right answer to make an important decision.

Never stop talking to each other and never go to bed angry. Your bed is neutral ground. No one person is in control. It is where you both get to show how you share and express your love to each other.

Love has no room for anger, especially if you want a loving marriage. You have to be strong enough not to always be the one with all the right answer. She has a right to give her input also and so do you.

In our relationship we don't have any set rules. We had to play everything by ear. We never scull each other for their mistakes. Mistakes are there to make things better by learning from our mistakes, so we don't make them again."

"So honey, when did you two discussed all this?" "Oh, we've had conversation like this for the past year or so. He would call me when he was on deployment. Just like his dad we skype and most of the conversation was done right here in my office. I knew by the way he was talking the direction and conversation were headed. He was thinking about marriage but, not this soon." I asked, "Why am I always the last one to know?" "Not this time, I think Trinity's parents are the last to know."

He then got up and poured us another glass of wine. I then asked, "So what he had to ask you, this now?" "It's something that should only be discussed by men to men." "Oh, it's like that" "No my darling" as he leaned over and kissed me, as he handed me my glass "You'll find out soon enough."

He then strikes a match as to light a fire and said, "Val, when you love, really love someone or something for that matter, it's like life's eternal flame that burns deep in your heart, eternally. That love is a flame that never goes out. No matter what or who comes in your life, it's there forever. You can never forget that love and that love will never let you go. You, my darling is that eternal flame that I can never let go nor will it ever burn out in my heart."

I then said, "You my darling husband are a true romantic. You also are my eternal flame. I can never let you go with words like that, my darling. Shall we go to bed?" "I thought you'd never ask."

CHAPTER
Three

We woke to the smell of SOS, Daniel turned over and said, "Soup's back." We got up and went down to breakfast. DJ and Trinity joined us on the patio. Daniel asked Soup when he got in. He said, "About midnight when you all were sitting out on the patio. I came through the garage. It seems y'all had a pretty important conversation going, so I went straight to the apartment. Asia and Diego heard me come in. They followed me to the house. I figured by now you two were tired of eating out or eating each other's cooking." I said, "We love you too Soup."

He then said, "Well, it seems like we're headed for another wedding," as he looked at DJ and Trinity. They both smiled and said, "Maybe." DJ asked, "Is it alright for Uncle Bernie to take us up to see Trinity's parents today? We have to be back on duty tomorrow." Daniel replied, "You need to get with Bernie and Jim, I have no control over that anymore. I could give him a call and see what their plan for the day. It's Saturday and this is usually down time for them. We don't have anything until Monday as far as business." Daniel excused himself and went to his office. He came back and said, "Bernie said he'll set a flight plan and get back with us."

DJ and Trinity left later that morning in order to get back to Fort Lewis. Daniel and I found ourselves during the usual on Saturday for the past year, Daniel in his office, and I up in my room working on my next book. I looked around the room and my eyes began to well at the thought of how much Q-tips presence was still in that room. I misses him so much. His spirit was all through that room. I got up stood, as I looked out my window that over looked the front of the mansion.

I heard the door slowly open from the adjacent room. Daniel walked over to where I was standing and said, "Let's take a ride. You need to get out this room for a while. I can see you still have not gotten over Q-tip yet." As he placed his arms around my shoulders and had done some many times before and said, "It's so very hard baby to lose that one you love so very much, Q-tip being such a huge part of you."

I said, "He became that part of me from the very first time I laid eyes on him. I believed he was preparing me for his death. I notice the strange things he used to do. I used to have thought about which one of the three I would lose first. I had a feeling it was going to be "Q". I believe he knew it also he and "Dee" would spend time together more than they usually. He was preparing to die and for "Dee" to take his place when he was gone. "Dee" would start to hang under me and he began to show more compassion for me and not as much for Asia as he used to.

The day it happened it was one of my usual afternoon picking up the girls from school. Krystyna was at home napping with her mom. Q-tip was happily waiting by the door to go meet Trinity at the school. We got in the car with his leash on. I pulled up at the school.

He was so excited to go see the kids and Trinity. By some strange but tragic coincidence he heard the neighbor's dog bark and he dash out across the street in traffic. A woman in a black SUV was driving above the speed limit and texting while driving.

She ran over Q-tip and didn't stop until she heard me yelling and others around. I couldn't do anything. I ran out in the street where he was laying and he was trembling and I picked his trembling body up in my arms and I felt his little life slowly leave his body.

I laid on top of him in the middle of the street and cried and scream as if that car had hit me. Some people came over to me lying on Q-tip and covered him with a blanket a woman had in her car.

By then the woman that hit him had gotten out of her car after stopping about 30 feet up from the accident. She was a Jewish woman, trying to sound very apologetic, as if it was a toy she just ran over, and said she didn't see him.

One of the regular guys whom were sitting in his SUV yelled, "You were texting, that's why you didn't see him." I was ready to kill her. I even threated to do so a couple of times, for killing my baby.

There were no other cars moving in either direction and she was in a hurry and was texting. She rolled over him Daniel, and said she didn't know she hit something. I told her, "If you had rolled over a rock you would have felt it. The dog was bigger than a rock. I called her a bitch and told her to get out of my face before I kill her.

Daniel I still wanted to kill her. She stole from me a very big part of me. All she said was I'm sorry I didn't know. Daniel it was a twenty miles an hour zone, a no cell phone and no texting area, in a school zone. She ripped my heart out of me and was about to leave it on the street in the middle of the school zone where children could see.

Daniel, I hurt so bad I can't get over this. This hurt is so deep and painful. I can't think and I can't breathe it hurt so badly. I pray to God please removed this pain and hurt in my heart but it's still there. It just won't leave. Help me Daniel to get over this pain and hurt. I loved that little guy so very much. It's like the core of my soul has been cut out of me. I can't sleep knowing he's not beside me.

I was crying so hard I was slowly sliding out of his arms and on my knees to the floor. He was still holding me and sat on the floor with me and rocked me as I cried and cried and said, I miss my baby so much, I miss my Q-Tip so much. If only I had made him stay at home with the other dogs, but he loved the kids at the school yard so much, and they loved him.

He said, "Just cry and let it go babe, this has been so rough on you and you have been holding this back for so long. I know you are hurting because you have not been yourself. You have been in so much pain and all I can say like you told me just let it go until you can't cry any more. I'll be right here with you."

He set there and rocked me until my cry turned to a wimple. I was in so much pain from holding it back for so long. As we sat silently rocking back and forth, he broke the silence in a very soft tone, "Val, remember the puzzle when you methodically broke it down to me about each piece and how it represents one's life.

You said, that one's life is not over when a piece of it is missing. Honey, your crew is that part of your puzzle, when it comes to your life. You need some closure when it comes to Q-Tip. A very precious and dear part of your life has been snatched from you and it's tearing you apart. I know you blame yourself for the whole situation that happened. There is nothing you could have done.

Try to understand, you're the one that said you believe "Q" was preparing you for his demised, as well as the other members of the crew. They knew the relationship you had with "Q" and I believe they felt your pain.

You later took Asia and Dee over to where the accident happened that night and how they were howling and whining over the spot where it happened. It started to rain and later that night a hard rain came through and washed the blood away.

Afterward, remember how they stayed under you and Dee always wanted to sleep with you or in your lap. He knew you were mourning for "Q" and was trying to comfort you. I believe they were more aware of his demised then you were giving them credit for. They hurt just as much as you do but they don't show it the way you do. They miss "Q" also, maybe just as much as you do but you can't tell it, especially Dee.

They had a very close relationship when you're not around them. They're even closer now since "Q's" gone. They loved each other and they lost their brother "Q". The one who always put calmness in the group. "You notice that too," I said. "Yeah, especially since I been around the mansion a lot, they would come out and sit out on the patio since DJ's not here.

I would talk to them and they would turn their head as if to listen or understand what I'm saying. I've grown very fond of the crew since they've been here. After all, they are a part of the family and I miss "Q" most.

I miss his presence and his candid look when he's up here. I hope you knew he was ruler of the upstairs. He did not allow Dee or Asia, for that matter, to come up here. This was his domain." We both laughed. I asked, "You notice that?"

He said, "I did. I also noticed you're suffering from PTSD. I been wanting to say this to you for a while now. Since that tragic accident, but I had to wait until you were ready. I had to wait until you were ready to let it go, as you once said. I think you have." "I have."

He stood up and took both my hands and helped me off the floor and said, "Good, that's my girl" "I still miss him so much," as I looked at Daniel. He gave me a big hug, as he rubbed my back up and down, and said, "I know honey, it's going to take some time, but you're strong and a survivor. You will get through this and I'm here for you." I said, "Thank you honey, and I love you too."

Changing the subject, "DJ called they're back at Lewis. They haven't set a date yet, but they do want to know if they can have the wedding here at the mansion." I said, "That would be just wonderful, to think this house will have seen three weddings since we been together"

"So, I gather by now you don't think the house is too big for us?" "I never thought that it's perfect. You knew what you were doing when you built this house. Another wedding and Charmaine and Jim has a baby on the way, our little family is steady growing. One day you will be a great grand pop." He said, "And you a great grand-nana" we both laughed." I said, "You so silly."

Daniel cell rang, He said, "Excuse me", as he clicked on the phone. He walked out the room and said, "She did what?" He went over to his room and kept saying, Um hum over and over and over. Where is she now? I'll be there as soon as I can."

He came back in the room and said, "It's Janelle" I asked, "Now what?" "She's trying to leave the clinic. She packed her things and setting in the lobby of the clinic waiting for me to come get her or she's going to leave on her own."

"So, you're going up there?" "I have to. I got to see this thing through one way or the other. After all, she's the mother of my children and she doesn't know what she's doing" "So, what cause her to want to leave this time?" "She's refusing some new treatment"

"So, she's refusing to let them continue to experiment on her with this new treatment." "I don't know honey, Janelle can be very difficult." "Daniel, I know you are right about that, but honey, don't you think she's tired of being that clinic's pin cushion? I know I would be. Those so called treatment has got to be painful to her. We don't know." "Honey, I don't know, Bernie and I are going up in about an hour. I just got off the phone with him."

"Ok, honey just be careful. But understand this, it's been over a year and she could be tired of all this. You know her better than anyone. She may be ready to give it up although you feel you need to do everything in your power to keep her alive because she's the mother of your children.

Don't make her suffer because you feel you owe her something." "Ok, honey I get your point. I got to go. I'm meeting Bernie at the hangar. I'll give you a call later." He came back and gave me a kiss and said I'm gone.

Daniel finally called late that evening and said he'll be back sometime tomorrow. We're on our way to Seattle. I said, "I gather you couldn't get her to stay?" "No, but we'll talk later, I love you" and hung up.

Daniel called and said he was trying to get Janelle settle back in her place. He getting her some help but she's being her usual difficult self. He should be in late tonight.

Daniel finally got in later the following day. He looked very tired and worried. He took a hot shower and laid on the bed in my room. He said let me get a quick nap and we'll talk." I sat there and watched him and walked out the room.

I went up to check on him and he was not in either room. He was down in his office going over some papers. I knocked and walked in. He said, "I was just going over some old papers." "What's going on honey?" "Janelle is just giving up. She's more mean and cantankerous as ever. She just wants to be left alone.

She has friends who want to help and she talks to them so cruelly. She doesn't want anyone to help. The last thing she said to me was get out her house and let me die alone. I don't need anyone's pity and she was drinking when she said it. Val, I think she's trying to kill herself."

"Honey, she's not killing herself, the cancer is, she just helping it along. She's ready to go but she's just being the only person she knows how to be." "DJ called and said Grandma called him and said she needed to see him. He's going over to see her later today. He said she doesn't sound very good.

He said she kept calling him Daniel Jr. She thinks I'm daddy. She said she needs to see me as soon as possible. I'm leaving work now. She doesn't sound good at all. I'm going back up in a few minutes. I was hoping you would go." "If that's what you want. I'll be ready, just let me get a few things together."

Bernie flew us up. It was a very quiet trip. Daniel was working on some papers and me, just staring out the window at the clouds. I had a feeling this was not going to be a good trip. When we got to the hangar DJ met us. He was still in uniform. He said, "See, you guys made it."

He gave me a kiss and his pops a big manly hug. Daniel asked "How things going?" DJ replied, "Pretty good, I haven't been to grandma yet, I was waiting for you pops. I'm not good at those things" He said, "That's ok son, I'm here now."

When we got to the house, it was a very large white brick house. I was very impressed with the structure. Daniel said, "Now son, if she thinks you Daniel Jr. let her think that. The doctor said she may be a little delusional. It maybe her medication and a combination of alcohol, so go along with her."

Daniel and DJ went in the house as Bernie and I waited in the SUV. I said "Bernie, I imagine we're not one of her favorite people." "I've never been." "Me either." We both laughed. He then said, "I've got to give it to my Dan. He has stood by her through this whole ordeal. I think it's taken a toll on him." "I know it has. It's got him very worried." "I've got to give it to him. He's been good to her no matter how bad she treated him.

He's a good hearted person no matter how bad that situation got." Daniel came out the house and said for us to go to the hotel and they'll take one of the cars and meet us there later. I asked, "How is she?" "She's talking to DJ, she thinks he's his father they had a very special relationship. I've gotta go back in. We'll talk later."

We checked in our hotel and I had Bernie to drop me off at the mall. I had to find some form of relaxation. I hadn't been in Seattle since I left Madigan Medical Center when I got Medivac back from Iraq.

Daniel met us at the hotel when we got back. He told us, "She's about the same but she's getting weaker. I can tell it in her voice. She thinks DJ is Daniel Jr didn't want him to leave. He's still there with her. I'm very impressed with our grandson. He has a lot of compassion and he's become a very impressive young man.

She has change since I left the other day. She has not cursed me out, not once." DJ knock on the door as he came in. "How things going honey?" "She's about the same. She keeps asking for you pops maybe you better get over there." "I think you better get back over there" I agreed, "I'll take a quick shower and go back over" "I'll go back with you pops."

Daniel went and showered. I asked DJ, how he's handling this. He said, "Nana, I not sure about all this. I have not been around a person dying like this. I feel so sorry for her. She thinks I'm daddy and she kept apologizing for being so mean to him and Auntie Danielle.

I told her we love her and we understood how she acted sometimes. She asked me to call Auntie Danielle. I called her and they talk for a while. I told Auntie Danielle she thinks I'm daddy so just go along with what she saying. She's a little delirious from her medications.

I don't think she realize daddy's dead. She asked how long she been this way. I told her the past few days. Nana, she called me when she was at the clinic several times, asking me to come take her home. These people are trying to kill me. She said she think grand pop is in on it." "You know that no true." "She said she think he's got another woman, because he keep leaving for days and then only come stay for a little while."

"DJ, it's probably her medication that has her in that frame of mind." "Nana, I know pops been nothing but wonderful taking care of her." "Your grand pops has been worried sick worrying about her medical condition. He has put a lot of airtime going back and forth trying to make sure she gets the best of medical care."

"Nana, you don't have to explain, pops and I have had a lot of conversation about grandmother. Way before she got sick, I know everything." "So, that's why you two are so tight"

He offered, "If I had to say I have a best friend that person is pops. He taught me everything I needed and should know as a man. Pops told me about the night my daddy died and what he went through.

He told me why my daddy was rushing back when he died." "He told you that?" "He told me that so I would understand how people can make mistake when they got love one on their mind. That's how my dad died, he was thinking of me. It wasn't my fault, things just happens."

Daniel walked in and asked, "You ready son?" "Yes sir." Daniel gave me a kiss on the top of my head and said, "I'll call you later." I smiled and said, "Ok."

Daniel called and said Danielle got in about an hour ago. She's staying at the house. DJ said he'll stay here tonight. Val, she hasn't been taking her medication. It's almost as if she's wants to die." "Isn't that what she told you?" I asked Daniel, "Where you at now?"

"I'm sitting in the car. I had to take a break from the atmosphere in there. Val, it's as if she wants us all to feel guilty about her condition. I just wanted to tell her you did this to yourself by not taking care of yourself. Don't blame us for what you have done to yourself."

I could hear him trying to not cry. Val, this is the woman whom I loved and trusted with my two most precious jewels. Now she blames us for what has happened to her. All she wants is to blame us for what she didn't do for herself. What's making me so mad, is what she's doing is working.

She's making me feel guilty for not being there for her, guilty of my infidelity and indiscretions. It's as if she's trying to make me angry enough to get her upset. She wants to blame me for her death." "Daniel, honey, get yourself together your two children need you there. Don't let them see what she is doing to you.

Just lay your head back and take a couple of deep breaths and get yourself together, I'll call you back in a little while." He said I love you and hung up.

I went next door to Bernie's room and knocked on the door. I said, "Bernie I need you to go over to Janelle's. Daniel is falling apart. I would go over there but I would definite be out of place. I know if anyone can bring some sanity over there would be you.

Daniel is setting in his car believing it is his fault that Janelle is sick and he is about to do something. I need you to go over there and try to set things in order. By the way Danielle is there too. I know Janelle planned this. She might be dying but she's not dumb." "I'll go over there but I don't know what I can do." "I don't know either, but do what you do best put some order in that situation." He grabbed his keys and left.

I waited about twenty minutes after Bernie left and called Daniel. The phone kept ringing. I heard the phone click on and a voice in the distant and Bernie knocking on the window. I kept yelling Daniel open the door. I heard glass break and Bernie voice in the distant saying hey, boy what you doing, trying to kill yourself with the car running.

He said no man I must have fell to sleep. Bernie said not with the car running, you know better than that crap, Dan. Get out the car and get some air. I heard Bernie ask, what the hell going on here?

I heard Daniel say "I was just resting my eyes for a minute. I laid my head back and I must have dosed off." "With the car running Dan, man this Janelle thing has got you all messed up in the head. What's up with this, talk to me, you know we can talk about anything." "I don't know Bernie. It's like this whole thing is all my fault."

"That's bull crap Dan, just like it used to be when you were in high school that woman got your head all messed up. She could say anything to you and you believe it or go along with it. Get your damn ass together, you are better than this. You got a wife and family who loves you and is worried to death about you. You cannot let Janelle's dying or death destroy what you have. She can't have you but, she's willing to destroy you one way or another.

She couldn't have what you have as far as love, family and what you have made of your life she is trying to destroy you. The one thing she has always had control of, you. Even with a beautiful strong wife like Val, you let Janelle destroy that, on her dying bed. Oh, hell naught.

Get your ass together or I'll kick it for you." "Alright man, I'm straight" "You damn better, you got a wife that's worried to death about you." Sounding confused he said, "I got to call her. What you doing here anyway?" "She told me she thought you might be in trouble, and for me to come check on you. Good thing she did. Dan you got a good woman, don't let Janelle on her dying bed destroy that. I mean it man."

I heard the car door open and closed, I hung the phone up. The phone rang, it was Daniel. I said, "I was about to call you back, you alright?" "Yeah honey, I dosed off a little, Bernie knocking on the window woke me up. I'm about to go back in the house. I'm going to stay here for the night if you don't mind." "No, just be careful." "I will, I love you" "I love you, more" and hung up.

Bernie called me and said, "Good thing you told me to come over here" I said, "I know I heard everything, he left the phone on when I called him back. You saved his life again. Thank you Bernie, I don't know what we'll do if you weren't around. I heard everything you told him. You are a hell of man and a damn good brother.

You have the voice of reasoning. I don't know how to thank you." He said, "All I can say, it's true all about you and your discernment. It was working this time. Daniel is a very lucky man. Just don't give up on him." "I won't, thanks again" "I'm going to hang out here a little while and then I'll head back." We hung up.

I had dosed off for a while, the phone was ringing. It was DJ, "Nana where's Uncle Bernie, I called his room and they said he was gone." "He's over there, I sent him over there about an hour ago. What the matter DJ?" "She shot at pops and me and told me we were lying devils.

She said she knew I was not her DJ, you don't look or act like him. She shot thru the door and missed me." "Where's your grandfather,

DJ?" "Last I saw him he was setting with grandma. I went down to the kitchen and that's when I heard a shot." "Your Uncle Bernie is over there somewhere. He might be in the car outside.

Go check and keep me on the phone." "Nana the car's out here, but I don't see Uncle Bernie." I heard a voice in the distance calling DJ. I then heard a shot, "What going on?" He said, "Its grandma she gone crazy in there. I think she shot pops." I was yelling through the phone at DJ, "DJ, what you mean your grandfather got shot?"

He said, "I don't know Nana. Uncle Bernie just ran in the house." I said, "I'm on my way over there." What's the address?" He gave me the address. I got in the cab and gave the address, as we pulled up to the house the fire department was arriving. DJ came over to me as I got out the cab.

I asked, "What the hell is going on here?" "Grandma tried to burn the house down with them in there? Uncle Bernie ran in to see what happened to pops. He told me to stay out here when he saw the smoke and flames. I called the fire department and that's when you arrived. I haven't seen or heard from pops or Uncle Bernie?" "Where's Danielle?" "She's at the hotel she had Uncle Paul to pick her up. She said she couldn't stay in this house it has too many bad memories.

Auntie Danielle and grandmother had some bad words and she left. She said she promised herself, she was not going to set foot in that house again as long as her mother was alive. If it wasn't for Paul she would have never came here in the first place." I said, "Ok, Danielle's safe, but where's Daniel and Bernie?"

By now the bricks were following from the house as it continued to burn. I heard a slight explosion from must had been gas. I was beginning to panic. I thought to myself that beautiful house gone up in flames. I noticed Bernie over talking to the police. I went over to where he was.

He excused his self and said, "Dan's gone to the hospital and Janelle. I'm on my way over there." As, we got in the car, he continued, "He's going to be alright he just has a flesh wound. I don't know about Janelle, she was screaming something about I told him I was going to kill him before I die."

I said, "Oh, my God she had this all planned" Bernie said, "It seems as though she did. She knew she didn't have much time left. When Dan and I went up to get her, he told me that if they tried the treatment on her it wouldn't help. She was told this and said I want to go home.

The doctor told Dan, she didn't have long to live, it's just a matter of days. She may have known this. I don't know if she loved Dan so much or hated him to the point she wanted him to die also." I said, "It might be because of me." "It might be because of you.

Daniel would never tell you this, but he told me. She was dangerously jealous of you. She felt you were the one who broke up her family and put a curse on her husband when he was in the Army. She hated you Val and it had a lot to do with what a certain person, whom you may know, fed her.

Val, you know hate is just like cancer it will eat you up if you don't do something about it. From what I could tell she had a lot of that for you and that's because you loved the one person she tried to control. I mean she tried to control Daniel and I love my brother, but she was the one downfall that he had. He carries a lot of guilt because of that love he has for you.

The one thing I have to say about my brother is that he loves you more than life. He would die for you if he knew that would save you." I said, "I've known this since the last time she shot him. That's why I believe she planned this for one reason to kill Daniel before she died.

I don't know if it was a good think to insist Daniel help her when she shot him the first time. It makes you think was it the right thing at that time." "Val, I've only known you for only a few years. And for what I know about you, you have a heart of gold. You care about people no matter who they are.

If you hadn't put that guilt trip on Daniel in that hospital, I don't think he would have done as much as he has done for her, if it wasn't for that. You care about people and it shows, even if you may get the raw end of the deal. Well, here we are."

When we got to the hospital DJ was already there. He met us at the desk. I asked, "Where you grandfather?" "He's fine. He's waiting for the doctor to come out and talk with him about grandma." "What's the status on her?" "I don't know, but it doesn't look good."

Bernie went to look for Daniel. Daniel stood as we came up to him. I hug him and kissed his forehead. "How you feel?" "Like I been shot, again" as he smiled. His right arm was in a sling. I asked, "Does it hurt much?" "Not much, they gave me some pain pills."

Bernie asked, "What's the status on Janelle" "The last I heard she wasn't doing that good. They're giving her morphine for her pain and trying to make her comfortable." At that time the doctor came out "She wants to see you Mr. Howard, I must advise you sir she doesn't have much time so try to keep her calm." "I'll try."

"She knows her time is coming and she wants to be at peace." Daniel asked me to walk down with him, "I'm sorry Val, I got you in the middle of all this" "You have nothing to be sorry for, I convince you to do this, to help. In my heart I know this was the right thing to do, now go in there. I'll be right outside if you want me."

As he walked in, I could see Janelle was no more than skin on bones. She was so tiny. Tears filled my eyes and heart as I looked at her. She was all but gone. I knew it was a matter of moments before she would pass on. I watched Daniel as he walked in her room and I felt his pain as he stood by her bed and ask could he sit. She barely had the strength to say yes.

He sat on the side of her bed and held her hand. He told her, "Janelle. I've loved you for so long and I'm having a hard time letting you go. You are the mother of my children and I don't want you to suffer any longer."

She barely could speak, but her words were painfully spoken "I loved you so much and I don't want you to see me like this, so I want you to leave and let me go in peace." He said, "I can't, I've come this far I'm going to be right here with you." It was silent for a good while and then there was no beep of a heartbeat.

I heard a soft cry coming from Daniel as he said, "Rest peaceful my love, I bid you farewell." He stood up as the nurse and doctor came in and said "She's gone." I went in and said, "Come on honey, we got to go, let them take over now." We went out to the waiting room where DJ and Bernie were waiting. I looked at them and said, "She's gone."

We all went back to the hotel and broke the news to Danielle. She took it very hard considering how she had left the house upset. It was daylight outside and none of us had gotten any rest. I went in to the bed room where Daniel was, he had taken off his sling.

He was still in deep thought of Janelle's passing. He then said, "Well it's all over now. I guess I have to prepare for the funeral. I'll have her body flown back to New Orleans. You know that's her home?" I said, "I know."

I asked, "Are you ready for this?" "I just want to get her back home where she belongs with her people. Have you ever been to a New Orleans funeral with the Second Line Band? It is something to be seen." I said, "Yes, I have during my time there after Katrina.

I'm fully aware of the way New Orleans have funerals." I then asked, "Are you alright?" "I'm alright. I just need to get through all what's been happening. I just need a little time. If you would only bear with me."

He continued, "I need to start working on those arrangements as soon as possible. I'll escort her back home." I went out the room and asked Bernie to go talk to Daniel he needs to get some rest.

He came back out about a half hour later and said, "He's lying down." "What did you tell him?" "I'll fly Janelle body home. That made him happy. I'm going to be there anyway for the funeral.

I'm going to fly you back home tomorrow, since there's no need for you to stay up here now. We should be back in a couple of days. I need to get Daniel straight. I told him I was flying you back tomorrow. He agreed." I said, "Well, I'm glad we got that all straight."

Bernie flew Danielle and me back to El Paso. We arrived about noon. Jim picked us up at the hangar and Bernie fuel up and headed back to Seattle. I got to the mansion and the crew met me as usual. Charmaine was at home and we talked about what had gone down in the past days.

I told her Daniel will be home in a couple of days and he would probable expect us all to attend the funeral in New Orleans. Two days later Daniel and DJ flew in. He said he was headed back to New Orleans to finish up the funeral arrangements.

We later all flew down to the funeral. Diane did not want to ride in the company plane with us. She claims she has a fear of riding in small aircrafts. The funeral was short and fast. Daniel and Danielle and her three grandchildren were together and I sat with Charmaine and Jim.

They did the second line dance after the burial and everyone danced coming from the cemetery except for Diane. We all ate and later flew back home. Daniel, Eloise and Bernie visited with old friends and family, afterward they all flew back to El Paso.

CHAPTER

Four

It's been a few months since the passing and ordeal with Janelle. Daniel was still trying to put closure on Janelle's personal business. She had a small will where she left everything to her friend Diane, even the house which was burnt out ruins. Daniel had that demolished a few days after the fire.

Diane had a stink about implying he had no rights to destroying her house her friend left her. She was informed by her husband the house was never Janelle's, it was Daniel's and he let her live in it. So, you cannot will something to a person if it's not yours.

I gathered that put a more bitter taste in her mouth about Daniel, being she believed it was all Daniel's fault Janelle was not taking care of herself which lead to her death.

Eloise and I had become very close friends. She informed me about how Diane felt about the house and Daniel for that matter. I told her don't worry about Mrs. Douglas as she insisted Eloise calls her, since her husband was her boss. Eloise had to politely inform her.

I do not work for Mr. Douglas. I work for CSM, my brother-in-law for that matter. He is my boss and your husband and I are a team which CSM put together. So keep in mind this is a family oriented organization and I hope you would keep that in mind as you continue to do your meddling, which you do so well."

"Diane is a chatter box. She has nothing to keep her busy so she gets into other people's business. Since Janelle's death she has no one to talk bad to about Daniel. If I know my Daniel, I know he's aware of her shenanigans." "Maybe we need to find something to occupy her time. I'll have a talk with her and see what she likes to get involved with."

"Val, it's been a long summer, the holidays coming. It's not our place to find something to keep Diane busy. She just needs to mind her and Tom's business. Daniel has made them both very comfortable lifestyles. Tom has his work to keep him happy and busy.

I just think we should leave Diane to Tom. He's been pretty good at shutting her down when she gets out of hand. I just wish he could keep her out of the office maybe we could get more things done." I said, "Don't let her get to you girl I know you can handle it, we'll think of something." I then hung up.

Daniel walked in the room as I hung up the phone, "What you two up to?" "It's not us, its Diane she still mad about the house." "Well, she just has to stay mad. She is one person who never gives up on anything she thinks she has a right to.

I'm not going to waste my time even discussing the matter. That's just how Diane is." "She's mostly mad because you had it demolished." "Val, what was she going to do with burnt out ruins?"

Changing the subject, I said, "Daniel, when are you going to tell me the rest of the story, that's not like you? We used to talk about everything." He said, "Well, it is about time I tell you the rest of the story." I asked, "What happen after you hung up from talking to me and went back in the house?" "I went in the house and Janelle was giving Danielle a lot of hell about how she abandoned her when she got sick.

Danielle was trying to tell her she didn't know she was sick. She was never one to go see a doctor. She called Danielle a selfish little uppity bitch. Danielle told her mother she did not come here to listen to her blame us for what she did not do for herself. She did not have to listen to her ramping and rudeness. She called Paul to pick up and he came and got her.

In the meanwhile, I had walked in on the conversation. I tried to calm Janelle down and got her back in the bed to rest. DJ came in and asked what was going on, that's when Janelle went off on DJ.

She said you're not my Daniel Jr. You tried to fool me and act like you was him, you don't even look or act like him. He would never let his sister talk to me like that. DJ told her I never told you I was my daddy. You just assumed I was and I went along with it.

You called me and asked me to come and get you. You the one called me to come see you. She said I just wanted to see if you were really my DJ and not that phony son of his.

I told DJ that's ok. Don't argue with her that's what she wants. DJ left the room and went downstairs. I went back in the room and Janelle had got out of the bed and was in her closet. I asked her, what was she doing? She said none of my damn business she was looking for something. I told her to get back in bed, I'll look for it.

She cursed me out again. Evidently, she found what she was looking for. She came out the closet with a gun in her hand. I asked her what she was going to do with that. She said finish what she didn't do the first time. Kill me. I kept saying Janelle put the gun down as I walk towards her.

I knew she was getting weak and the gun was a little heavy for her. As I got closer I snatch the gun from her and she fell back. That's when it went off as it fell on the floor and she grabbed it. That's when DJ came to the door and she was yelling telling him he was not DJ because he didn't act or looked like him. I grabbed the gun again it went off and creased my right arm and hit the bedroom door.

I fell back and hit my head on the dresser and knocked me somewhat dizzy. I tried to get up and I saw Janelle lighting a candle and setting her bed and clothes in the closet on fire. I yell to her what was she doing. She said, I going to kill us both, I'll burn this place down with you in it. I know you brought that bitch up here with you.

That's when I heard Bernie at the door trying to get in. He told DJ to get out and call the fire department. She kept saying I'm going to burn in hell and you going too. She kept screaming at me with her weak voice you son-of-a-bitch. I kept saying, Janelle don't do this.

Bernie bust the door open and grabbed me. I told him to get Janelle, I'm alright. She was fighting him trying to get loose. He carried her outside with her screaming. You know the rest of the story. Now Diane thing is that she thought she was going to get Janelle's house after she died.

Now this was supposed to be her friend. I brought that house for her just before we divorced so she had a place to live. It was my house I let her live in it not Janelle's. Janelle has never worked a day in her life. I have always taken care of her.

She never owned a thing. I gave her everything. She had nothing to give or leave to a single soul. She didn't even have an insurance policy. I had that if anybody had anything it was I.

She hated me in the end but I loved her and I took care of her. If she wanted something and needed something she asked me. I was always there for her and she knew it. All Diane was to her an information channel when it came to our relationship. She was never a real friend.

Val, I know Janelle loved me in some selfish distorted way but, I knew her well enough to know she did not know how to love. At least not the way two people in love care about each other. She was more about what she could get out of me and how she could get it.

I felt more sorrow for her than anything because she didn't have anyone but her grandmother who loved her. Janelle's mother abandoning her made her the way she was, a user and I let her used me. I left her, but I knew she needed me. She had no one and she ran everyone who cared about her away like Daniel Jr. Danielle, and little DJ.

All she knew was how to run people away who loved her. I really think Janelle hated herself more than anything. She never knew real motherly love or how to accept it. She was never taught that by her mother. She never accepted her grandmother as her surrogate mother, because of her hate for her own mother leaving.

Val, this bothered me for years not understanding why Janelle was the way she was. I just finally gave up on her when I met you and fell in love with you." "Well, honey that's all behind you now and you has done your part. You have a lot of people who loves and care a lot about you. Look at what you have accomplished in your life.

You still have your work and your many projects. We have a new grandchild on the way and a wedding to plan coming one day. Our life is full. Most of all we have each other for eternity. How do you feel about all what has happened?"

"I'm glad it's all over, and she's not suffering any longer. I just don't feel content about the situation. It's got me feeling lost and empty inside like I didn't do enough." "Do you still feel guilty inside and why do you feel this guilt?"

"I just felt I abandon her when she needed me." "Abandon? Ooh, I understand now, that's the hold Janelle seem to have had on every one of you. She wants you to feel y'all abandon her, when in reality she ran y'all away.

That's her hold on you. She made you feel guilty after making you leave her. So you, could try and make up for leaving her. Subconsciously that gave her all the right to reject anything and everything you did to make up to her.

She wanted to reject your forgiveness. That was her pay back and her intent to her mother, if she had ever showed up again. She was out for revenge to anyone who showed her forgiveness; even you, my darling husband. All she wanted was her own personal revenge.

This is something she could never do, make her mother pay for or make up for, leaving and abandoning her. So she makes people who love her pay for what she never got from her mother. She was a sociopath it was always about her. It was never about her love for you. It was more about you paying for what her mother did, than what you were forced to do.

Remember the conversation you and Bernie had outside the car when you fell to sleep and he had to break a window. Well, I heard the whole conversation. But the main thing I heard him say, just like it used to be when you were in high school that woman got your head all messed up. She could say anything to you and you believe it or go along with it. She's got you still doing the same thing.

She said you abandon her and you feel guilty enough to believe it. She forced you to live with all her accusation and assumptions. Diane fed the fuel to the fire because you felt some guilt about our relationship.

The worse part about it, you were happy and that made you feel that much more guilty. You felt guilty because you were happy and tolerated all the drama that went along with it. Honey, that was almost twenty-five years ago. How long was she going to make you suffer? She wanted to make you suffer and pay for it until you or she died, if she could.

The worse part about it, you are allowing her do it even from her grave. How long are you going to let her make you feel guilty about finding true love and happiness? It's tearing you apart. Don't let her do this to you or us. You are making her the winner in this. She's making you suffer and she's dead and gone and you still have a life to live. We have a life to live together."

"You're right, I never really thought about what was happening. I was only thinking about what I was doing wrong and I had to fix it." "Yeah, Mr. Fixit, you don't always have the tools to fix everything that you think needs fixing."

"Bernie told me you heard the whole conversation we had outside the car. He also told me you were working overtime with that gift of discernment you have. He said you are a very strong woman and I do not know how lucky I am. Believe me, my darling wife I do know. You have the wisdom to take a situation and break it down and analyze it to each minutia detail.

I am so impressed how you figured out why Janelle was doing what she was doing." "Believe me honey it was not easy, but I kept hearing this about people who loved her was abandoning her. She was hung up on this thing about being abandon. I just couldn't understand why she was so stuck on that one issue.

Then it dawn on me, she never got over her mother abandoning her. She felt everyone who claimed they loved her would eventually abandon her and when they did she was never going to forgive them. She was never going to ever forgive y'all. All she wanted was to reject that forgiveness. I was just thinking did she feel the same way when DJ died. Did she feel abandon by him?"

"Maybe she did, she really did hated me at that time. She actually blamed me for not being able to save him." "Well, I finally realized it was not so much as being abandon, as it was being able to let the one who loved her know she did not forgive them; and she wasn't going to forgive them.

Daniel, I believe she was never going to forgive you for leaving her. If you had ever gone back to her, she would have never let you live that down. This was all about her unforgiving.

According to the Bible there's no moving on without forgiveness. That's probably why she couldn't move forward she was not able to forgive, those who trust past against her, especially her mother."

I continued, "Bernie told me something that stuck in my mind, He said, "Val, you know hate is just like cancer it will eat you up if you don't do something about it." She must really hate her mother for what she did. I just think if she only had forgiven her, she may be still living and happy.

On this trip, I really got to know my brother-in-law these past few days. I know now why you depend so much on him. He is the voice of reasoning and he is your strength in critical situation. I'm glad you two found each other." "Huh, me too!"

Just as we started to walk out the room my phone rang. I said hello, and old voice out of the past said, "Hey Valeria Elizabeth," I knew right away who it was. I said well, I be damn, Elaine Hartley where the hell you been, It's got to be about fifteen years since I heard from you. How did you find me?"

"Well you know when you in the Army you can eventually find anyone you looking for." "Where you at now?" "I'm down in San Antonio as the Brigade Command Sergeant Major." "You still in recruiting?" "Hell, yeah, you know I don't know how to do anything else. I'm retiring in about six months."

"So, how did you find me?" "Your grandson's in one of my stations. I ran across him when he was in recruiting school. I was there giving a talk on recruiting and that's when I met him." "So, you met DJ my grandson?" Yeah, he's a pretty sharp soldier. We talked awhile. He told me you married his grandfather a retired CSM and y'all live in this huge mansion down in El Paso."

"I wouldn't say that it's huge, but it pretty big for the two of us and we got the dogs and family. You must come down and visit us. You and Daniel would have a lot in common. He loves the opportunity to talk Army." "I'd love to. I understand you'll a big time novelist of love, romance and drama?"

"I've written a couple of books and they're doing pretty good. I'm not one of those starving writers. But, that's enough about me, come down and spend some time with me so we can do some real catching up.

I would love the company. I would love for you to meet my husband Daniel. He's the most wonderful person in the world." "I going to take some time off in a few weeks, maybe I'll give you a call then?" "That would be great, now don't you forget? It's so good to hear your voice after so many years. I got your number now so we can talk more often." We then hung up.

DJ called me a few days later and said he was at his new duty station in San Antonio, TX. He said his brigade CSM was a CSM Elaine Hartley. She was on her retirement tour and was beginning to transition to civilian retired life. I told her my grandmother used to be a recruiter at Fort Sheridan.

That's when she told me you two were best friends for years. Y'all went to recruiting school together and then to Chicago Recruiting Battalion. She said y'all recruited there for about six years. You went to California and she went to Georgia. I told her you a well known published author now and you live in El Paso with her husband my grandfather.

She said she was going to give you a call. I told her I had planned on getting married in a couple of months. My Nana loves to have weddings at their mansion. I gave her your number and she said she was going to give you a called.

Nana did you know that she's gay?" "Yeah, she had her moment when we were on recruiting together. But it was never a problem for me. She did her thing and I did mine's and her thing was never my thing and it never interfered with our close friendship.

You'll find out recruiting is a very close net group. We played and party hard but, it was always about the mission. We had an old saying "Make Mission, Go fishing".

Not trying to change the subject but, did you say you're getting married in a couple of months." He said, "Yeah, we're thinking about around Thanksgiving. That's when most of our friends can come up for the holiday and don't have to worry about taking leave and we won't have to take leave." I asked, "What about your honeymoon?" "I have that all figured out."

"Well, you better let Soup know something if you planning on having it here. He has the regular holiday festivities to prepare for also." "Trinity and I are coming in next weekend and have a meeting with you. Trinity's parents will be flying in also." "I'm glad you're giving us some time to know this.

I'll get with Soup for the dinner. Have Trinity give me a call so we can have things set up the way she wants it. It doesn't have to be nothing fancy just Charmaine, Jim, Trinity's parents and you and Trinity and your pops and me.

Well, looks like we're going to have another wedding and a very busy holiday coming up. Make sure you call your grandfather and let him know what's going on." "I already have. He told me to give you a call." "Well, as usually I'm the last to know." "No Nana, not this time mom and Jim is." "Ok, I don't feel so bad this time, Have Trinity to call me, I love you."

I then hung up. Daniel walked in and said, "I gathered you've heard the news?" "About what?" "Now don't be coy with me, you know what I'm talking about." "Ooh, you mean the wedding." "Yes, I mean the wedding and my grandson asked me to be his best man."

"Oh, that wonderful, y'all like to keep it in the family with this best man thing." "I guess we do." "I guess that means you're going to do it." "Yes, I am." "Now that we're going to have a dinner to meet Trinity's parents, I just think we should invite them to stay here at the mansion.

This way we can get to know each other better." "That a great idea, but Val this is not your opportunity to probe into her family." "Daniel, you are not going to tell me you have not already looked into her parent's background."

"No, I have not and I am not going to." "Well, that's a first." "Val, I thought we been over this before. If she's good enough for our grandson to fall in love with, then it's none of our business what or who her parents are.

Those two young people are deeply in love with each other and that's all that matters." "Now, that we got that straight. I have a close friend an old recruiter buddy who may be coming for the wedding and also for a visit.

She's DJ's brigade CSM and she's gay." "So, what does that have to do with anything? One of my best friends and buddies I grew up with is gay and is in the Army.

Remember Chaplain Anderson who did our wedding, he's gay. I found that out when we were in high school, but I didn't really know until I was in the Army and he told me himself. He told me he felt it was his place to tell me if someone else would spread rumors about him.

I told him I knew this back in high school. I asked him have I treated you any different since he's known me. He said no, so what makes you think by telling me makes any difference, now. We've been best friends since we grew up in the projects. Nothing will ever change that.

So, you have a close friend who's in the Army and she's gay. Well, that makes two of us." "Well, I just thought you should know." "Well, now we both know. We both have friends in the military that are gay. It's something that has always been a part of military life and it's been kept a secret for many years. So, why are we having this conversation?

Now we're no longer has to hide the fact that many of our comrades has different preference and they make up what is a big part of the military. I have always accepted it as a soldier and as a Command Sergeant Major. It doesn't make me any less of a man or person.

Some of my best soldiers in leadership position were gay and I was proud to serve with them. I have a few working in my company now. They are damn good at what they do.

Being that your friend is a retiring CSM I'm very anxious to meet her. What's her name?" "Elaine Denise Hartley" "Think I might have run across her doing my time as CSM and the academy. The CSM is a small community when you think about it. They eventually run across each other at the various conferences and back at the academy." "If you did you definitely would remember her."

"Well, since we got that settle think we should break the news to Soup about the wedding and all." "Yeah, he loves it when the house is giving a celebration." "I was thinking isn't it time we had an anniversary party. We've never had one since we've been married." "Well, this is no better time to bring this up to Soup.

You know he's been working on getting his catering business started. He's got the staff and we can give him a lot of business in the future."

Soup was doing his usual thing in the kitchen as we walked in, "Well what do my two most favorite people have going on that you bless me with y'all presence?" Daniel said, "You know it's getting to that time of the year when we start our annual celebrations.

This year may be a very busy one for you. First, I want to ask you, how you coming along with your catering business plan." He said, "To tell you the truth I've had a little set back because of my past credit history. So, I may not be able to start that business."

Daniel said, "Man, why didn't you tell us this? How long you've known this?" "Oh, about several months now, no bank would lend me the money." "That's bull. I'll lend you the money." "CSM, I don't want you to lend me the money, I want to do this on my own." "Soup, don't think of it as me lending you the money. Think of it as an investment you'll be the sole owner.

We can talk about all this later, let's say later today. You and I will set down in your office and go over what you showed the banks. We'll do this in your office mine can be somewhat intimidating to some people."

"Now, that we got that settled we have a few projects we know you can handle. You know DJ and Trinity are getting married. As a matter of fact it's in a few or should I say a couple of months.

We're talking, the Thanksgiving weekend. Trinity's parents are coming in the weekend after next for the wedding party's get acquainted dinner. I'll get with you later on who those guests will be attending.

Now keep in mind there's the regular Holiday Festive party and Daniel hasn't and won't mention, (I winked) for New Year's Eve's we been married going on four years and he suggested we have an anniversary party and marks his retirement from the company. So, then there's the baby shower for Charmaine and Jim. So, my dear friend you have a lot to keep you busy for the next few months.

You're going to need a lot of help and what a better way to start your new business. I am so excited." "So, CSM, Miss Val, you're not doing this because we're friends?" Daniel replied, "No man, you're family and plus you the best caterer in El Paso. I couldn't think of a better place to invest our money. So let me know when you want to set down and go over all this. So, what're you going to name your company?" "**SOUP'S KITCHEN** Catering Service" "I love it, it's perfect," I agreed.

"Well, you two have a lot to discuss and I have some things I need to do also. Charmaine and I are going to get some things for the baby's nursery." Daniel asked, "You need a driver?" "No, Jim's going to take us. I'll walk over to their place it's just a couple of housing down."

I was very happy that Charmaine and Jim brought the house just a few doors away from us. That way it kept the family close and Danielle and Paul lived a few block over. As I walked out the house I called my best friend Jai, "Hey girlfriend what you up to?" "I'm about to set up a teleconference with your husband in about an hour." "Teleconference"

"Now, Val don't get all riled. He's more of an advisor." "Um hum." "Who knows those countries better than him and Bernie? We've got a pretty big job coming up in Afghanistan once the draw down starts, and who knows those people better than him. So, he's going to advise us on some things, not as a participant.

How is he doing since the retirement? This new position he manage to talk me into has kept me from the mansion. I don't get to see my people anymore." "You know I miss you girlfriend." "I miss my best friend too."

"I'll tell Daniel to get Bernie to slow up on those contracts so you can spend more time with us. I called to tell you DJ's getting married over the Thanksgiving weekend." "Oh Great, it's about time."

"Also, Soup's got some great news for you." "What my buddy up to, I don't get to see my friend or talk with him much anymore." "He's had a lot on his mind lately but things are turning in his favor."

"Last I talked to him he had some disappointments about starting his catering service. He then went on vacation to New Orleans and I haven't heard from him since. He's alright now?" "Yeah, things couldn't have been any better." "Well, I better get back to work before my boss calls me."

"How is it with Bernie in charge now?" "Same Ole, same ole. He's just like Daniel. He more laid back. He let us do our job and don't get involved unless we ask or he feels he need too. He's just like Daniel. We really got to find some time to talk. I'm dying to hear about the drama in Seattle with poor Janelle."

"Girl we need a lot of face to face on that story. When you coming to El Paso? You got those two jets make an excuse to come visit me." "I will, I got to go my land line is ringing. Love you girlfriend," and hung up.

I had reached Charmaine's and Jim's place. They had a beautiful red brick four bedroom house. I rang the doorbell and walked in. "It's me." "I'm in the kitchen." As I walked in I gave her a kiss and asked, "Are you sure you not having twins, you look mighty big for six months?" "No Val, Danielle said he going to be a big boy like his dad and brother DJ."

"DJ's not big, he's just very tall, and it runs in the family. Where's that husband of yours?" She said, "Speaking of the devil" as he walked in. "Hey, Miss Val." As he gave me a kiss. "I pulled the car around whenever y'all ready."

"He's going to drop us off. You know he's not a shopper." "That's ok, just like Daniel would rather sit back and watch the shoppers than shop. You ready?" Jim helped her up and carried her purse as we walked to the SUV.

"DJ called and said they've set the date, the Saturday following the Thanksgiving holiday. Have you notice Val, we tend to have weddings tied in around special holidays."

Jim said, "Valentine wasn't a holiday." She said, "It was for me." "It was for me too" as he kissed her hand. I thought to myself, I'm so happy for my friend. She has been through so much these past years. Things are just about to change for the best for the both of them.

I could see they are so much in love with each other. As I laid my head back to enjoy the short ride to the mall I thank God for giving me a wonderful family that I love so dearly.

We arrived at the mall, Jim got out and helped Charmaine out the SUV, I asked "You sure you feel up to this?" She said, "Sure, I need to walk instead of staying in the house watching TV. We're just going to a couple of stores." Jim said, "I can stay and wait for y'all?" "No honey, I know you have some things you want to do."

We look around and brought some things for the baby. Charmaine said her back was bothering her and she was ready to go. I called Jim and he said "I'm right here at the mall. I went to the book store and decide to wait for y'all. I'll pull the car around to the entrance." We met Jim at the entrance to the mall. He suggested maybe we should go by Danielle on our way home. We agreed.

CHAPTER

Five

Danielle saw her right away. Danielle came out and told us, she was a little concerned. She explained, "Jim I wasn't too sure about this the other day when y'all were here for her checkup. Remember I told you I thought that was another heartbeat. There is another heat beat.

Y'all are having twins." I asked, "How is that so it doesn't run in either of your family." Danielle said, "I don't know but let me tell you about this little guy or should I say little girl. She was hiding behind her big brother" as she spoke she started to cry. "That happens sometimes with twins.

The strongest or the biggest seems to protect the weakest or the little one in the womb. That's when you only hear one heartbeat. I believe this is what happened in this situation." I asked Danielle, "Are you alright" as I rubbed her back. She said, "I am now, I just realized something. I'm going to be alright. I just remember something.

When you and Charmaine decide to have a baby, I had suggested that she try fertility pills and she did but they made her stomach upset so she stopped. Maybe she was pregnant then. I believe this is why she's having twins. This could be the only reason if twins didn't run in the families."

Through the whole ordeal Jim was smiling knowing there were going to have twins. I was so shock and happy I didn't know what to say. Jim went in the room where Charmaine was. I asked Danielle, "You were thinking about you and Daniel Jr. weren't you?"

She said, "I was, but I can't talk about it now I have patients coming in for appointments. Can I stop by later tonight and talk to you and pops. I have something I need to get off my chest." "Sure I'll make sure we'll be there, we have no plans tonight."

Jim dropped me off before he and Charmaine went home. I ran in the house where Daniel and Soup had finished their meeting. I was so excited I didn't ask them how things went. I kissed him on his forehead and started rambling off what had happened. So, I got to the part where we took Charmaine to see Danielle.

I said "Honey, remember I told you Danielle thought she heard a second heart beat but it could be the baby had gas. It wasn't gas. It was a second baby. It is a baby girl. She was hiding behind her brother.

Danielle believes he was protecting her because she was the weakest." Daniel commented, "How is that so, twins don't run in either of their families?" I said, "I know, but Danielle had suggested Charmaine take the fertility pill because they had decided to have a baby.

They made her sick so she stopped taking them. But, evidently she was sick, but from the pregnancy. Now, with all that said, Danielle wants to come by and talk with us if she can tonight after she gets off. I told her we'll be here.

I then got myself together and apologized for interrupting their meeting. Daniel said, "Oh, we're finished. We were toasting to the new owner and sole proprietor of "Soup's Kitchen Catering Service"." We're going to check out some Real Estate tomorrow." I asked, "Don't you have a teleconference to do today?"

He asked, "How you know that? I postponed it for later today. So, how did you know?" "I talked to Jai earlier." "No, I'm not going to Afghanistan or anywhere. We got too much going on here." "Ok, I'm going to hold you to that." "If you two future grandparents excuse me I have a few calls to make."

Daniel and I got up and walked towards the upstairs. I asked, "So how much did you invested?" He said, "A half a million. That's only

$500,000." "So, what's the difference between lending and investing?" "If I lend him the money he'll always feel he owe me something and if he defaults on the loan I lose out. If I invest in it and it faults or fails, I come out ahead. I can take his business from him and the bank loses. Then I can give it back to him as a gift.

I would never lend the money to Soup. Not because I don't trust him, but because he means too much to us to insult our friendship by having him to pay on a loan. On one that someday he may not be able to pay back.

So as an investor, he owes us nothing but to show us a profit in his business. You see investment is all about profit. So how did you make the bank lend him the money?" "What I did I told Soup give me the bank who told you the worse reason why they wouldn't or couldn't lend you the money.

He gave me that bank. I took the number and went into my office and I talked with the bank's president. I told him who I was and what my worth was and the amount I am willing to invest in this company. I told them I personally have faith and vouch for this man's ability to pay the loan back.

He verified my worth and called be back and told me Soup have been approved for a half million dollars loan. He will go and sign for the loan tomorrow and I will not be there with him. He will do this on his own."

"So what about the loan? How is he going to pay that loan?" In December I will pay off the loan tell him the loan was paid off through his investors?

Then the only people he has to please would be his investors which is you and I. We are the sole investors and soon to be him and DJ in "Soup's Kitchen Catering Service." "Damn, you are a damn good businessman."

"I learned by asking the right questions, just like you? If you don't know how else are you going to find out without asking the right questions?

That's why I asked Soup to give me the number of that bank that gave him the worse reason why they wouldn't give you a loan. I had to show that penny Annie bank that Soup was no Joe blow asking for a loan to get turn down by some small branch loan processor.

He was a man who had a dream and was looking for help. That man told him we don't finance those types of loan to minorities. That is why I went back to that bank and made sure tomorrow he will go up to that same loan processor and let him know he got the loan even though he is a minority wanting to get a loan."

He then said, "Well, I did my part shaking up the system because there's no room to help minorities with their dreams." "I asked, "So what is your worth now?"

He said, "Hell, I don't know somewhere short of about five billion in assets. I really don't try to keep up with it. I just make sure I have enough zeros to use it when I have to. It's not something I can take with me if I died today or tomorrow.

When Danielle said she was coming by?" "She said after work, she got all choked up at the clinic when she was telling us about Charmaine's them baby girl hiding behind her brother. It brought tear in her eye and she had dificult in telling us about the position of the baby.

I think it made her think of her and DJ. I guess as twins you never get over losing your twin or the other half of you. She may still be struggling with that. You know she took it pretty hard when Janelle died. Do you think a lot more happened in that house than she told you?"

"I don't know Val, but we'll know soon enough she just pulled up in the driveway." "Is she by herself?" "Looks like it. This must be pretty serious if Paul's not with her. He may be out of town they got that new contract with the draw down coming up." We heard the doorbell and her voice saying "Hey pops, Val it's me" Daniel answered back, "We saw your car pull up we're on our way down."

As we walked down the stairs, we could see she had been crying and she was still a little upset. Daniel said, "We're about to eat dinner in a short while, why don't you stay and eat with us." She said, "No, I told the kids I had some late appointments I'll bring them some pizza for dinner."

Daniel gave her a kiss on her forehead. He put his arms around her as we walked to the family room. "Now, what's so important that you needed to tell us about tonight?" She said, "I don't know how to tell you pop's but, I wanted to tell you that night we took our walk. I just want you to know mama was evil. She did some evil things to me and DJ. She did it mostly to DJ."

Daniel looking somewhat befuddled asked, "What kind of evil stuff she did to DJ?" "Pops she made him sleep with her when she was drinking. She would come in our room and tell him mama's scared I need you to protect me.

DJ would ask her who's going to protect Danielle. I need to protect Danielle. Pops want me to take care of Danielle. He wants me to protect her. She used to say if you don't come and protect me I will give her to the gypsies.

He would say ok mama I'll come don't give her to the gypsies. He would then go to her room. I would go listen and I would hear her saying things to him as if he was a man. She would force him to do things he didn't want to. She told him if he didn't I will kill your sister. Don't think I won't I've tried it before. You know I will.

This was around the time we tried to find where you were but we had to come back to the house." Daniel said, "Wait a minute, you mean to tell me all this was going on and I knew nothing about it."

"I wanted to tell you many times when you came home, but DJ told me not too. Mama said pops might take us from her and she'll be left here alone. So, let's not tell pops about it. Mama is sick and she needs our help. That was a lie. Mama wasn't sick she was just doing sick things to DJ at the time.

Whenever DJ refuse she would do mean things to me until he agreed to what she said or wanted. She burned me on my arm with the poking iron and that's when she told you I was very clumsy I tripped over the stool and my arm hit the stove. Another time she cut my hair because DJ said I'm not going to do that anymore mama.

She grab me by my hair and told him if you don't I will cut every piece of hair on her head. That's the time you came home and saw I had cut my hair and she cut it.

She told you I wanted my hair like the girl on TV so she tried to cut it herself. I wanted you to take us with you every time you came home and mama would act like she's this great mother of the year."

Daniel was putting his hand over his face and shaking his head. He looked up with tears in his eyes and said, you been holding this inside for all this time." He took a deep breath and said, "That's why Janelle came down after we had that walk. Did you tell her I knew about her and DJ?"

"No, I told her that I was going to tell pops everything, everything you said about him and everything she did to DJ in her bedroom. I told her that I was going to tell him how you treated me and what you did to me when DJ wasn't around and how you try to make me sleep with your boyfriend who like little girls.

I told her I hated her more than I ever hated anything in my life. She told me on the phone I don't care because DJ loves more than your daddy because he does anything I ask him to do. I told her DJ doesn't love you. He loves me more that's why he did those things to you so, he could protect me (she started to cry uncontrollable). She said, that's a lie DJ loved me because he told me. I said mama DJ is dead let him rest in peace. She hung up and that's when she showed up here.

Daniel got up and poured us a glass of wine. He gave us our drink and said, "Val told me how you got a little upset at the clinic today." She said, "I did, all this time I held this in and when that little baby girl showed her head today around her brother all I could think of was my brother, the way he protected me all those years.

He would always say Danielle I will always protect you. You my twin we are just like one. He would say I won't let mama hurt you. But she did up until the day she died. Mama didn't love DJ she just knew how to manipulate him. That way was me.

She used me to get at you pops and that was through DJ. When DJ fell in love and got married. She went crazy and broke up everything in the house of his. When he got killed she took what little she had left and took it to the back yard and burned it.

She said I hope you burn in hell. You went and got yourself killed just so you won't be with me. She called him a son-of-a-bitch. I cried for mama but it wasn't because I loved her. It was because I tried to love her and I felt sorry for her.

The only thing she knew was how to hurt the people who cared about her. Now here it is two months after her funeral and she still has a hold on us. Pops, I'm thirty-five years old and I still don't know who my mother was. She was a very strange and evil person is all I knew."

Daniel said, "I know honey, one day when this all calm down I will tell you about your mother and why she was the way she was. I prayed for her soul because she did have some evil ways." He took a deep breath and said, "You want to call that pizza in before you leave." "I better, I didn't mean to take up all this time, but I'm glad I did. I told Paul this years ago before we got married.

I remembered when DJ died, Paul told me, I'll always be your knight in shining armor. He married me with all my wounds and scares." Daniel said, "You got a good man there treat him right. I knew that the first time I met him. Now go home to him and your family." We walked her to the door and Daniel walked her to her SUV. He gave her a kiss and watch as she pulled around the driveway and left.

As I waited for Daniel, Soup said, "Dinner's ready. I asked, "So Soup how you going to do this, are you planning on giving up your job?" He said, "No Miss Val, I'm not planning on giving up my day job until I get loaded like you and CSM." "I'm not loaded, it's CSM who's loaded." "Oh, my bad!" We both laugh. "When the last time you talked to my best friend?" "I just got off the phone with her about a minute ago." "Well looks like we're going to have a very good end of the year.

Now when do you want to get together reference that wedding party dinner?" "Let's do that tomorrow after you handle your business. I sure like to be a fly on that wall when you walk in that bank."

"Why don't you, I would love the company. They don't know you that rich guy's wife." "I think I will." Daniel walked in "What you two up to?"

"I'm going to go with Soup to the bank tomorrow, just to see the look on their face when he signed that loan contract. I'm going to love this." "Val, behave yourself." "I'm going to be on my best behavior." "Let's eat. What's for dinner?" "Spare ribs." "I thought that's what I smelled." We all headed to the kitchen.

I could tell Daniel was still upset by what Danielle had told him. I asked him, "You going to be alright?" He said, "Yeah, It's all behind us now. Danielle told me she didn't tell me this the night of our walk because you might have done something really bad that night." "Who knows what you would have done the day she showed up here.

If you can remember you were ready to fly up there and throw her in the street. That was nothing compared to what you know now. I think we all are very fortunate you didn't know all this than." "Val, the way I feel now, I know I would have killed her. She would have blamed it all on DJ, that's just how crazy she was."

"I'm trying to figure this out, where was your head when this was all going on. I can't see you being an ostrich with your head buried in the ground. You were always gone. You knew who you were married to. How in the world you not notice anything in that house. Was your mind just on the military? You knew she had problems and you over looked them, way before I came in your life.

Those things didn't show up when I came along. They were there way before we met. They wanted to be with you and you just kept thinking about how lonely Janelle would be without the kids. A damn pervert, when all she wanted was to keep that boy with her so she could continue to molest that child.

The more I think of what she forced that child to do because she knew he would do anything to protect his twin. Lord, please forgive me but, I'm glad that crazy bitch is dead. I hope she burn in hell.

Why were you always thinking about Janelle's feelings? She mistreated you for years and you put up with it because you were feeling sorry for her. A person can take abuse only for so long. I know that from past experience. I'm mad about this whole thing. I don't want to say this but, you should have taken those kids way before you met me. They would have been better off with you in the military."

He finally said, "I know Val, I have gone over this in my head the last hour. I am so mad at myself. I have no idea what made me think she was a good person to look after our children, when I knew, how she treated her grandmother and the way she treated me.

I just need to put her out of my mind. You know she's probably setting down there in hell just laughing at how much we are still talking about her. We have got to let it go."

"Yeah, honey, you right. But, I just can't help thinking about what those kids went through and all they only had was each other."

Daniel got up and pace the floor for a moment. He then went down to his office. He called later and said he was going by Bernie's. I figure that's where he would head. Bernie is being the only other person who knew crazy Janelle just as well as he did. Here we were, that woman lay rotten in her grave and she still had a hold on this family.

I said **to myself out loud "Lord, give us peace. Heaven knows we need it after this mess."** I got out the shower and dressed for bed. My thought went back to my little companion as I fell asleep.

CHAPTER Six

Soup and I went to the Bank to sign his loan contract. The loan officer was sitting there looking as proud as he could to greet us as we approached. Soup introduced me as one of his colleagues. The loan officer was very cordial.

After signing the papers as we began to leave I informed the loan officer, "I'm sure we will be doing more business with you in the future." He informed me, "After all we do support our minority future business owners." I replied, "I'm sure you do, now" and walked away holding Soup's arm.

As we pulled into the drive way Daniel was coming out the door. I asked, "Where you headed?" As he open the door and helped me out the SUV. "I'm taking a walk." He questioned, "What you two been up to?" "We just come back from the bank, signing the loan contract." "I know, the Bank's president just gave me a call. He said everything worked out just fine. I told him I'm sure it did and thanked him." "I know he did."

"Val, what did you do or should I ask what did you say?" "I just told the loan officer I'm sure they are willing to support future minority businesses." "That's all you said?" "Well, I gave him a little "Diva attitude" on the way out."

"Well, I guess you made your point, he wants more business from us." "That's your expertise I'm just the Diva with an attitude, honey." We both laughed. He gave me a kiss, as he walked down the driveway.

"I won't be long. Oh, your future daughter-in-law called, she'll call you back later."

As I walked into the house, my phone rang. It was Trinity, "Hey honey, I just walked in the house." "I just want to fill you in on the situation with my family. You know my mom and dad are not married anymore. Dad's remarried and mom lives alone in Chicago."

"Okay, I'm somewhat aware of that. So, do you think it's going to be a problem with them here?" "No, Miss Val, it's just that my mother has gotten over the divorce but, I don't think or should I say my stepmom hasn't gotten over it. She tends to be somewhat a little jealous of their relationship because of me."

"So, what you are saying there may be a problem?" "I don't know and I hope not when I told daddy about the wedding planning dinner. He called and asked me were your mother coming. I told him yes. He said, well, you know Eva is not going to let me come alone.

I told him I expected both of you to come. So, to make a long story short I wanted to give you fair warning about my mother and stepmother." "So, is your mother coming alone?" "So far she has not mentioned anyone." "Well, we'll be prepared if she does." "I wouldn't worry about that, Daniel seem to let the steam out of situations like that pretty quick.

Your father being a retired first sergeant, I'm sure he can handle those two ladies." "Did I mention my mother was in the Army also, and so was Eva." I thought to myself *'this is going to be interesting.'* "I appreciate your enlightenment. Just keep in mind, dear this is all about yours and DJ's special day. I'm not going to let anyone mess that up for any reason. Just remember this is all about you and DJ, no one else."

Changing the tone and subject, "Have you and DJ decided what type of wedding you want to have?" "Right now we're kind of set on a military wedding with the mess whites for the men and sabers. I'll be in white bridal gown. I haven't picked my colors yet because of the military and I need to get with DJ's mom because we want her to be the event planner for it. I heard DJ's Aunt Eloise did an excellent job on yours in a short amount of time. I would love for them to be the planners."

"You need to keep in mind DJ's mom is very good at what she does but, you do realize she is going on seven months pregnant with twins. She can do the planning but the labor will have to be done by her assistants. By the time the wedding she will probably be ready to have those babies."

"I didn't know she was having twins, does DJ know yet?" "I don't know but, she was going to tell him today. She just found out yesterday. Well, have DJ give me a call when he gets a chance." "I will I'm meeting him in about an hour." We hung up. Daniel walked in just as I hung up, "So what you two young ladies are up to?" "I'm not sure yet but it's going to be a very interesting getting acquainted wedding dinner party.

I don't know if it should be called a dinner party." "What done happened now?" So, I explained the situation between the mother and the stepmom. He said, "I don't see a problem in this at all. Trinity's father should be able to handle this if it becomes a situation. I'm pretty sure it won't.

They all are professionals and career minded people being that they all were in the military at one time. Trinity's father knew it would eventually come to this one day. At least it's on neutral ground. I just think you are a little overly concerned about nothing." "Alright, but at least I've given you heads up about the situation." "I got it, and if it does I will make sure the right person will handle it."

The following weekend DJ and Trinity came down to help set up for the dinner party. I still was a little concern about the ex-wife and stepmom being in a face-off. I was not going to have that going on. Charmaine and Jim came over to help supervise the setup.

Charmaine informed me Danielle had suggested that she go on total bed rest for the remainder of her pregnancy. This would mean Eloise and with my help would handle the wedding planning. Charmaine would set in on the meeting with the family and help with the invitations and decorations. Eloise said she would be more than happy to take over for Charmaine.

Daniel and I took over the responsibility as the host for the special occasion. We cordially met our guest at the airport with DJ and

Trinity. Trinity's father was very slim and about the same height as Daniel. They hit it on very well. Trinity's dad, Antonio did the introductions.

His wife Eva was a quite attractive and somewhat laid back young lady. They had a set of twins also. Charmaine and Jim met us at the mansion when we arrived. They were very impressed by the beauty of the mansion as we drove up. We all went into the family room for get acquainted cocktails.

Later that morning Cassandra, Trinity's mom arrived. Trinity and DJ met her at the airport. Daniel and Antonio were in his office as they walked in. Eva and I were coming down the stairs, from showing her the house as they walked in. Cassandra was a very tall and slender very attractive woman. I could see from the eye connection there was somewhat of an unfavorable feeling between them.

Trinity introduced her mother to me. Daniel and Antonio must have heard her as they came out of his office. I figured Daniel had a conversation in reference to Antonio's ex-wife and current wife being in this type of gathering. The introductions were very civil. I took a deep breath and gave Cassandra big welcome hug. Daniel gave her a hug also.

Soup came in and announced lunch is being served in the dining room. We all walked in and got our plates and sit down. I could still feel some friction going on. I could see Daniel had noticed the same. As always, Daniel spoke first, "It is a great privilege to welcome our future granddaughter-in-law and her parents to our home.

We have gotten to know Trinity very well over the past year. We love her and already see her as a part of our family. We are here this weekend to make sure we give these two young people whom (as he looked at me, and then DJ and Trinity) a very beautiful and the type of wedding they want. So, again welcome to our home. Everyone smiled and said thank you.

The rest of the meal was spent in idle chatter back in forth around the table. I notice there were little conversation between Cassandra and Antonio and none between the two exes. This is something that has nothing to do with our children. I feel as long as we can get through this weekend things will be just fine.

After lunch we all went our separate ways. Antonio and Eva went to their room to get settled in, while Trinity went to show her mother their room she wanted to spend some quality time with her daughter whom she hadn't seen in a while.

Daniel and I retired to our room to get freshen up for the evening. I asked, "Couldn't you feel the tension in that room?" "Yeah, I could cut it with a knife. Now, Val I know how you are, this is not a concern of ours. We can't fix everyone's problem. Evidently, there are some deep rooted problems there and its Antonio's responsibility to work them out." "So, what were you two talking about behind closed doors? And I know you don't go behind closed doors just for chit chat."

"I asked Antonio, being that Trinity mom's is coming in. Was there anything I should be concerned about? He said no, you know how women are, for some reason if two women are in the same room with the man the other was involved with they tend to want to show their fangs to each other.

I told my wife Eva, this is for Trinity and DJ, whatever feeling you have about her mother I expect her to be civil in this whole matter. She agreed." "Yeah, but those claws were really showing when they met eye to eye." "I noticed that also.

He assured me he has control of this situation. He said this has been going on for years. They just don't like one another. Trinity knows this and is aware of their feeling towards each other." "So, if this is so why did Eva come?"

"To keep an eye on her husband you know how you women are. She doesn't trust him. So honey they are our guest and we must show them equal attention and no favoritism." "I agree honey but, it's really up to those two ladies to do the right thing by Trinity and DJ."

Daniel went over to his room to prepare for our guest and dinner party. I decided to take a nap before the party.

Daniel later walked back in the room and asked, "What you thinking about?" "I was just thinking, how Janelle treated her grandmother the way she did when she was growing up.

So, with that in mind, I think it's time we got ready to meet our guest for cocktails." Daniel went back over to his room and got dress. I took a quick showered and put on a pair of camel color slack and a cow neck pullover.

CHAPTER Seven

He knocked on the adjacent door and walked in. I asked, "Why do you knock on the door when it's only us in the house?" "Just in case you're not alone shall we make our entrance?"

DJ, Trinity and Cassandra were in the family room as we walked in. Daniel went over and offered everyone, what's their choice. DJ said, "We having yours and Nana's favorite." Daniel said, "Good choice." Antonio and Eva then walked in with Charmaine and Jim.

Daniel offered them a drink, they declined. He then said, "Shall we all retire to the dining room." Soup had done a fabulous thing with the dining room. He had two of his stewards serve dinner and waited on the table. The main meal was Cornish hen and spring peas.

Daniel again welcomed everyone to our home and then got down to business. He broke the ice and almost threw me out my chair when he mentioned, "I felt a bit of tension in the room, and as the host of this soon to be joyous occasion.

I want to express, this is not a time to bring up old wounds or any type of previous misconceptions or misunderstanding that may have occurred in the past. We are here to help my grandson, DJ and Trinity to prepare and give the most beautiful and joyous wedding ceremony they can have.

My wife Val and I are both retired military and we are very much aware that everyone in this room and at this table is retired or prior military.

DJ and Trinity has expressed to us they want to have a military wedding here at the mansion. We are pleased and honored to have the wedding here at our home." He then continued, "With that I now turn everything over to my grandson DJ and his beautiful fiancée Trinity."

DJ got up and thanked his grandfather and for everyone's attendance. He then turned everything over to Trinity who did the same. She informed them that DJ's mother who is an excellent and well-known event planner here in the El Paso along with his aunt Eloise Howard will be handling all the wedding arrangements and the ceremony for the wedding. What she would like is for us to get together and help her decide floral arrangement and the colors.

Daniel and I then got up and walked out. We felt it was an opportunity for the mother of the bride to get together on those particulars and we would get with Trinity later on what her decision was.

The following day our house guests left. It was a good feeling for us to be alone in the mansion. We found ourselves wanting to spend more time together. Our thoughts were still heavy on what Danielle went through those years she spent in the presence of all that went on in their home. Daniel didn't mention any of what he now know what was going on in his absence. I believe he truly think it was all his fault.

There is nothing worse than to finally find the truth of something horribly happen in your life and you feeling you may have played an unknowing part in the whole situation.

Daniel would sit at his writing desk in our room and just stare out the window in total silence and I could see his eyes well up and he would get up and walk out the room and often go for walks. I could see he was really suffering. The worse part of the whole situation is I didn't know what to do or say. I was afraid this would take a toll on him in more ways than one.

As time moved closer towards DJ's and Trinity's wedding, so did the time for the birth of Charmaine's and Jim's twins both brought a warmness to my heart. The sudden ring of the phone brought me back to the reality of what lies ahead. Charmaine was on the other end.

She was in total hysterics. In between her crying, I managed to ask her was she alright and was the babies alright. Daniel walked in the middle of my probing to calming her down. He stood in front of me and said, "Tell her we're on our way. Where's Jim?" I shook my head, to say I didn't know.

As we arrived at the house, Charmaine was standing in the door. Daniel helped her back into the house. Still trying to calm her down, I told her, Charmaine you have got to remain calm think of the babies." We walked her into the living room with Daniel's arms still around her as he led her to the sofa. He took her hands and in his calm and soothing manner asked, "Charmaine what's going on? And where's Jim? Charmaine continue to try and hold back her tears and outburst.

I then got up to get her some water, as she tried to explain, "Oh Pops, I don't know where to begin," she paused and in a difficult manner continued, "About a month ago, a young lady, by the name of Anna, showed up at our door and said Jim was the father of her eighteen year old daughter. This was all a big surprise to him as well as me. She said her daughter is a student at USC. To make a long story short, she said her daughter has been missing for almost three months. Her roommate said, she went to a party up in Hollywood with some friends and haven't seen her since.

She said she went to the police and to the university and talked with security and they didn't know anything about her being missing. They told her students go on holidays and sometimes quit school and don't tell their parents.

She told us her and her daughter are very close and don't have any secrets. She would have told her if she wanted to or did quit school. She was so upset. She didn't think her daughter, Stephanie was dead, but had been kidnapped and maybe sold into white slavery.

Jim asked her, "Why should I believe you, after so many years?" She told him she was at her wits' end. She had no one else to turn to except him. He was her last results. She thought since he was still in the military maybe someone could help him find out what happened to their daughter. That's when she showed him the birth certificate proving he was the legal father of their daughter."

Daniel mumbled to himself, "Jim never told me this. We've talked off and on for the past few weeks, but none of this came up." Charmaine was much calmer now as she continued, "After Anna left, Jim I assumed, felt he owed me some sort of an explanation. I felt he didn't after all we all had a life before the one we have now. Well, he told me he met Anna while at Fort Benning, GA.

They dated the whole time he was there for Jump School. He was really involved with her. One day she told him her father was transferring and they were moving. He really cared a lot for her. They stayed in touch for a while and then she went to college and he hadn't heard a thing from her until she showed up at the door. He apologized for bring his past relationship into our home. I told him you owe me no apology we all had a past life.

After a few days went by, I noticed this thing was bothering him. He and Chief had a few conversation going on but he never discussed it with me. I knew they were up to something.

I guessed Jim decided he had to do something. He came to me one morning and said he and chief had a mission and they were leaving in the morning. He said he was sorry but he won't be gone long. He suggested I go and stay with y'all until they got back since I would be here along at night. I told him I'll be alright." She then started crying again as she tried to continue, "Then Chief came back and told me Jim had to stop over in LA and he should be back in a few days.

Pop's that was almost a week ago. I haven't heard from him; not even a Text or email. That's not like Jim knowing it's getting so close to the twin's birth. Pops I'm so worried about him. Jim has never done anything like this before." "I know, this is totally out of the ordinary for Jim. I need to make a few calls, if you excuse me."

Daniel walked out the room as he held the phone to his ear. I suggested, "Charmaine maybe it is best you come stay with us for a while. I know you want to be here when he gets back and everything, but I would not have a peaceful moment knowing you are here by yourself worrying about you here alone." Agreeing as he walked in, "It is not a bad idea for you to be around family for a while.

I know you want to be here, but it is for the best for you and the twins to be around us for a while. So, my dear wife why don't you help Charmaine get some things together while I finish this phone call." I saluted and said, "Yes, CSM." He winked and continued his phone call.

Daniel dropped us off at the mansion. I helped Charmaine get settled into her old room. I felt so much better having her back at the mansion with us. Daniel returned later that evening just before dinnertime. I went up to tell him dinner was almost ready and to ask him was there anything on Jim yet.

He said, "Chief and I are working on some leads." Sounding somewhat agitated by his statement, I insisted, "What you mean you and chief is working on some leads?"

He turned and looked at me as he tucked his shirt in his pants, "Babe, I don't mean to be short with you, but this thing has got me all uptight. It's just that I can't believe after all we been through together, I don't want to think the worse."

He reached in the drawer of his writing table and checked the ammo in his weapon before he placed it in his "To go bag" and continued, "Val, I can't tell at this moment until chief read me on it. I have no idea how serious this is but it is somewhat heavy stuff." "I figure that, you carrying your old standby, I haven't seen you pull that out since you were a contractor."

"I know honey, but I don't know what we're up against when we get to LA. I'll let you know, but I don't want you to tell Charmaine anything no matter how much pity you have for her not knowing. We must keep her calm and make sure you tell Soup that also. I'll make sure to pass that on to him on my way out." Daniel left later that evening.

The following evening Daniel called as he had promised. He informed me they were still chasing some leads that would probably end up as no luck. Chief has some leads that maybe some help on Jim's daughter's disappearance as well as his."

"So you are saying Jim's disappearance and his daughter's maybe somewhat linked." "No, Val, all I'm saying they may be tied in somehow together. All I can say Jim is alive. He has been seen but, where he is now is not known." "Well, that gives us some hope."

"At this moment, I know these could be some very treacherous and dangerous individuals." "Daniel you are scaring me." "Honey, I don't mean to scare you but, I feel you need to know, that people dealing in human trafficking is dealing with more than just people. They deal in drugs, weapons and maybe even human organs. There is nothing they wouldn't stop at."

"Daniel you be very careful. I know how much you love Jim, and you would do anything to bring him home. Keep in mind you have a family to come home to also." "I will honey, and I love you too. I'll call you on the phone in my office from now on its more secured."

Daniel and Chief took longer than expected. He called several time with just pieces of information to pass on to Charmaine. A couple of days later DJ called and said, "I got a call from Pop's. He wanted to know if I could meet them in LA. He said it was a family emergency and he needed my help. He didn't have time to give me the long version and to give you a call." I gave him the abbreviated version of what's been going on. He then asked, "How's mom and the twins doing."

"They doing just fine, you want to talk to her?" "No, I don't want to have to do any explaining to her and prefer she not know what's going on." "Well, that up to you, how's Trinity doing?" "She, doing great, she's going with me." "DJ you got to be kidding, what y'all up to? I hope those two brothers are not pulling you two into this mess. They are up against some very notorious people.

I can't believe he's getting you in the middle of all this." "He asked me to come. Trinity decided to go on her own. She said we are her family and she has all the rights to help if there is an emergency. Nana, when Trinity makes up her mind about something she doesn't let anything change it. Not even me. I won't and pops or chief will put her in harm's way. She's a hell of soldier whether you know it or not."

"I guess it's your call but I've got a few words for your pops next time we talk." "Ok, but he doesn't know Trinity's coming. He just said it's a family emergency." "Well, I guess he'll know when y'all get there." "Nana it's going to be alright.

You know pops and Uncle Bernie already has a plan especially if they asked me to help. Well, I've got to go I'm picking Trinity up in an hour. I love you Nana and don't be such a "worry wart." I'll give Trinity your love," and hung up. "Worry Wart," I mumbled as I hung up.

CHAPTER Eight

I didn't hear from Daniel until about a week later. He said, "We had a lead on Jim's disappearance. But Stephanie's disappearance is still a mystery.

We think she's out of the country. It's been months since her disappearance. We are very concern about her wellbeing. These kinds of situation can get very dangerous. The longer the person has been a prisoner or a captive it creates a form of Stockholm syndrome. I'm afraid she is a victim of white slavery and sold into prostitution.

It's a big thing in some of these countries. When they kidnap these young people and they wear out their usefulness they are often auctioned off, sold or even killed. Some are even so drugged out they are dumped off in some foreign country with no identity or means to get back home.

The worse part of this is if they seem difficult when first captured, it's usually when organ selling comes in play.

These young healthy people ends up in some hotel on skid row packed in a tub of melting ice without a kidney or so much as a heart missing resulting in death. We have come across those situations on several of our leads."

He continued, "Val, I'm very concerned about Jim and even more so about Stephanie. This whole thing may end up taking us to another part of the world. I may need you to stay in contact with Tom and Eloise at the COC.

I hope you don't mind spending some time over there. You would be better informed with what's going on from there. I've already updated Tom and Eloise about you being somewhat a part of the mission." "Ok, honey if that's what you wants but, just what am I supposed to be doing?

I really don't want to be away from the house with Charmaine being so close to her time." "I understand but you will only be away from the house a couple of hours a day. I also asked Jai to come down."

"Jai, Daniel what are you two up to?" "Val, I'm not sure what I'm up against, but I want to have Jai's extraction teams ready if I need them.

There may be a need for them on this mission. I just want to be prepared." "Well, I'll do as you ask it's probably the only time I'll get the best information. When do I have to be there?" "Jai is on her way there if not there already, she'll be your driver. I've got to go. Chief' them are waiting for me."

After talking with Daniel I went out to take Asia and Dee for a walk, as we came back to the house Jai was pulling up. I said, "Well it's about time you got here.

I was expecting you a while ago." "Well, I don't know why you thought that. You know how that husband of yours is. He calls and next thing I know, I'm on a flight to El Paso."

"Well, it must be nice," as we gave each other a big hug. "What is that husband of mine's up to now?" "As always he never really fills me in until the poop hits the fan.

All I know, it has to do with Jim's daughter. I didn't know he had a daughter." "We didn't either until a few days ago. This was round about the time he came up missing."

"Missing! Don't they have a set of twins on the way? I've been away too long." "Yeah, you have been gone awhile. You have a lot of catching up to do. Right now I need to get back and check on Charmaine. Just don't mention anything about Jim's disappearance. I'll catch you up on the rest of what's going on."

The following morning Jai and I reported over to the Command Center. Eloise and Tom were there when we arrived. "Well, it like old times again, welcome aboard ladies.

I assume Daniel has filled you two in on what's going on and why we're all here." he offered. I said, "Not really, last I heard there was a lead on Jim's status. Chief and DJ was waiting for him. After that I don't know what's going on." "Well Val, a lot has happen since your conversation with Daniel.

Daniel wants me to pass on to you and Jai. They've located Jim in some hotel on "skid row" in downtown Los Angeles. He was packed in ice in a bath tub." "Oh my God!" I said. "He's alive but his missing a kidney according to Daniel."

"What you mean missing a kidney, Tom?" I asked. "Val, Daniel will fill you in later but don't tell Charmaine what I just told you. Jim's in the hospital and will probably be released in a few days." "Missing a kidney and being release and then what?" I mumbled as I shook my head.

"Daniel them, are still looking into the disappearance of Jim's daughter and in the meanwhile Jim will be coming home." "Tom, now you know as well as I know, if Jim is anyway able to move around he is not going anywhere until he find his daughter." "I know, but that's Daniel's intent, whether that going to happen who knows." He exclaimed.

He continued, "Now the next leg of this mission is to find Stephanie and bring her home." "Have they located her?" I asked. Eloise offered, "We're working some leads through "Polaris" the National Human trafficking Resource Center. They inform the public about where cases of suspected human trafficking have occurred within the United States.

Polaris is one of the few organizations working on all forms of trafficking. They have been a big help in providing us leads in where Stephanie could be or have been. I'm saying this because it depends on who her kidnappers are.

We have very good contacts and leads, but we don't want to be on a wild goose chase. Every minute counts in these situations. All we know is that she went to a party in Hollywood thinking she was with a friend.

Eloise continued, "According to Polaris, these people deals in organ trafficking, a very organized crime, involving several hands in the pot beginning with, the spotter/recruiter, transporter, and medical staff, to include the middleman or contractors, and the buyers.

The buyers are who contacts the middleman or the so called contractors. Once the victim or donor is available the medical staff does their job in removing the organ parts.

The organ is transported by the transporter to the medical teams who surgically replace the needed organ into the recipient. The recruiter or as we know as the spotter spots and locate a donor. The majority of the time these are unwilling or unknowingly donors. Jim is one of those unknowing donors.

Tom added, "If it wasn't for the word and contacts Chief and Daniel had manage to put together in the homeless district in downtown LA they probably would not had found him.

If it had not been for the cleaning woman who found him in that bath tub packed in melting ice. Many victims don't survive this type of body trauma." "Jim was very lucky," Eloise added with tears in her eyes.

Tom continued, "Human trafficking is a multi-billion dollar trade. Unfortunately for Jim, the organs most traffickers seek are kidneys. Jim, being a healthy body, asking questions in the wrong part of town became prey to these organ seekers.

From what we have found out trafficking organs is a very lucrative trade because in many countries the waiting lists for patients who need transplants are very long.

Love ones and individuals are willing to pay any amount of money to keep them alive." "Does Daniel know all this?" I asked. "Oh, we briefed them on all this a couple of days ago." Eloise replied as she continued.

"Now what we found out about Stephanie, even though she is a very beautiful young lady, she did not have many friends or someone she could call her best friend. She went to a fraternity party one night and met a girl she was going to school with.

They hit it off pretty good and they became kind of close friends. Well this girl whom she thought was her friend was a spotter for this organization setting her up to become a victim of human trafficking."

"So what you saying this girl pretended to be Stephanie's friend and set her up to be kidnapped and probably sold into possibly the sex trade," Jai exclaimed. Eloise continued, shaking her head as to say yes, "We're afraid so.

They have what they call "spotters" who are very selective in the young people they take. Usually ones they have been watching for a while. Those that are somewhat quiet and mostly keeps to themselves. Eventually they make their move to befriend them.

The spotter invites them to a gathering. Let's say a party, usually their extraction point. They usually drug the pawn's drink or other means that could render them unconscious."

"So it seems this girl must do this a lot, that's where we are now," Tom added. "We have infiltrated their little so called set up at USC with our people and it has made some progress. I will not tell you who those individuals are, but I will say they are good at what they do." "Who are they Tom, is it DJ and Trinity?" I asked.

"No Val, Dan would never jeopardize their lives in something as dangerous as this. I will say it's a male and female team from another contractor who volunteered to take on the mission." "So where are we now on all this?" I asked.

"We are currently waiting for a SITREP from Chief and CSM. That should be in the next hour. They have their command center down in Seal Beach at an old Naval Station. Trinity is working their command center. She's pretty good at the command center detail." "I'm familiar with the area. I used to lived there as a recruiter." I acknowledged.

An hour later Daniel and his team gave us the SITREP and what their next move was. They were heading home to drop Jim off and heading for Rio de Janeiro, Brazil.

Brazil's a known source country for moving human and drug trafficking. It is the destination for trafficking of men, women, and children that are forced into the sex trade.

We have no leads but we do know this is a beginning or a start. This is a hunch and we have to follow that hunch. I believe that hunch is going to lead us to where Stephanie is. We have to be ready for whatever happens. That's why we have three extraction teams located and ready for deployment.

We believe Brazil is where they stage these Human auctions which are where they handles biding through online and close circuit TV for each of their trophies.

They usually have these auctions somewhere near the ports in a warehouse close by the docks. These trophies or contraband are held off shore during the auction biddings. Making it easier to move the contraband after the deals or bids has been closed. They either move them as freight cargo by ships or by air.

Once Jim gets there y'all will be monitoring these auctions from the Command Center. We have managed to intercept their feed for monitoring each of the bidding processes.

Once Stephanie is identified we will deploy our extraction team in the area to where she's being held or transported. Eloise did you take care of that package I requested?" "That's a Roger, CSM." As of this moment this operation code name is "Cobra Gold"." If you don't have anything else I'll see y'all in about an hour. 'Cobra Gold' signing out.

Jai and I headed back to the mansion to check on Charmaine. Just as we were pulling into the drive way Daniel and Chief was pulling in behind us.

Daniel got out the truck and walkover and kissed me on my forehead and hugged Jai. "Where's Jim," I asked. "Oh, we dropped him off at home." "Charmaine is here." I said. Jai went in the house as we continued to talk outside the house.

"Val, he wanted to go home before he came here" "Daniel, what's going on, is Jim alright?" "He's as well as he can be, if you call getting your kidney cut out of you and getting the hell beat out of you. Other than that I think he'll be alright.

He's got a lot going on in his head. He's been through a hell of a lot these last few days. Let's not talk about it right now. Don't tell Charmaine he went home."

"Ok Daniel, but you better tell me the rest of this story." "I will" as we walked in the house. The crew came racing down the hall to meet us. We acknowledged them and headed up stairs. Charmaine met us coming down the hall. She asked where Jim was. Daniel said, "They had to stop by the command center to drop off some equipment. He should be here shortly." She then turned and went back to her room.

We went into our room. Daniel went to take a quick shower. I asked, "So what happened?" He took a deep breath, hesitated and said, "When I got the word where Jim was, I was working on a lead up near North Hollywood.

It was a woman on the line. She asked if I was the person looking for the man on the flyer. I told her I was. She said she knew where he was. I asked, where is he? She said she was cleaning one of the rooms at the hotel where she works.

She went in the bathroom to clean it and she noticed a man was lying in the tub covered in ice. He was not breathing and he looked like the man on the picture on the wall down in the lobby. So she went down stairs and told the desk clerk and he called the police and the paramedics.

Chief was down in that area following another lead. I called Chief and told him I think they had found Jim. He's at a hotel down in the homeless district in one of the hotels down on skid row. I gave him the address the woman had gave me and had him meet me down there.

When I got there Chief was already there. The police had not arrived but the paramedics were there. We went up to the room where he was and the paramedics were trying to stabilize him. I asked was he still alive.

They said he was but looks like he's missing a kidney. I closed my eyes and lean back again the wall. He was all bruised up from the beaten he sustained in his face.

I had Chief to follow them to the hospital where they took him. I stayed back to talk with the police and to get some more information on how he ended up there.

It seems Jim got a call in reference to where Stephanie was. When he got there he was told to go up to the room and the man had information where he could locate his daughter.

When he got there he was jumped by a couple of big bouncer guys. They beat him really bad but they did not do any lower body torso injury.

These guys knew where to beat a person and not injure the body part that was needed. They then gave him a sedative that would instantly sedate or render him unconscious. This is, I assume, when they did the so called surgery and removed one of his kidneys.

I talked with the police and they told me this is not unusual. This is something that happens all the time in the area. They used these hotels as what they call "watering holes" where they catch some poor innocent victims looking for information or a place to stay.

In Jim's case he was asking for information. We think the desk clerk lured him down there about information they had to offer him and he was victimized and they robbed him of one of his kidneys."

"The police didn't do anything about it," I questioned. "No, babe no not really they are either in on it, or they may just don't care. Like they said they have enough trying to keep the peace down there.

When they get calls like this, they have to arrive on the scene, but most of the time the victim is already dead. Their job, as they informed me, is to get the coroner on the scene and do a report. They have at least one of these every day.

You got to understand that a dead homeless person don't mean nothing to these people or cops. That's just one less problem they have to worry about. The cop told me in a nonchalant attitude your son was lucky, if you had not posted those flyers with his picture all over the area you might not had never found him. It's probably the reward you offered and posted that you got so lucky.

They never pay attention to those things down here. Down here they just live their lives from day to day. These traffickers come through and offer a few buck and they jump on the opportunity to make a few bucks. There is a lot of crime down there and the innocent falls victims to it if they're not streetwise or careful.

Val, this is where I need your help, in reference to Jim. Through my somewhat observations, Jim is going through something.

Since you're going to be at the COC, try to keep an eye on him. You'll have to do this in your usual mother hen manner. I believe Jim may be suffering from PTSD.

He is very withdrawn from things that might or should be important to him. When we were landing he told us he did not want to go home yet. I asked him why, Charmaine has been worried sick over him. He said he wasn't ready to see Charmaine yet. I asked him why. He just said CSM, I 'm not ready to face her.

I just can't face her right now. He then said just drop me off at home. I told him, but son she at my house. He said I know CSM just drop me off. Chief said ok, Jimbo I'll drop you off first. After we dropped him off we could tell he was not his usual self. He usually so anxious to see Charmaine. Val, on the whole trip home he never mention her once.

Chief said as we drove off, that boy's suffering from PTSD. I said I think so too. I asked what you think brought that on. Chief said he's been through a really rough three months. He's been victimized, taken advantage of, finding out he has a daughter and no success in finding out where she is or who kidnapped her.

He has a lot on his mind and everything he's done to fine her has fallen apart for him. He's had a lot of disappointments and he's blaming it all on his self. This has affected his self-esteem.

I think having him run the operation from here is our best move for him. At least he'll know what's going on. It hurts to see him going through this. He is usually a very strong individual in times like this." "Honey, I suggest you talk to Charmaine reference Jim's current situation.

He's not going to want to tell her how he feels or what's going on in his head, mainly because of how he feels about his self." He took a deep breath and continued, "Right now as many PTSD victims are, they do not know how to fix their so called situation.

They withdraw from what's going on in their life and they start by rejecting and withdrawing from anything or anyone that is willing to help them like he did earlier today.

If this is PTSD, you will have to play a role in helping him recover from this. Working in the COC could be a big help for him also. He would need to still be in on the mix of what's going on."

"First you must make Charmaine aware of his condition. Also it would be to both their advantage for her to remain here with us until this is all over with.

Those babies could come any day now. Hopefully things will be better by then." Daniel finished dressing and walked out the room. I asked where he was going. He said he was going to talk to Charmaine.

Daniel stopped by the kitchen on his way out to tell Soup. Charmaine will probably have her dinner in her room this evening. I asked him how she was feeling. He said, "She's doing just find. She's much stronger than we give her credit.

She said he called just before I came to her room and said he was coming over after he take a shower. But, she knows something wrong with him she could tell it in his voice."

He then said, "I'm going by the COC, I'm pretty sure you ladies have everything in total control." He gave me a kiss and walk out to the kitchen shaking his head. I looked at Jai and said, "Things going to be a little rough around here for a while," "You right girlfriend and it going to affect all of us."

Jai and I left to go to the mall for a couple of hours. When we got back, I asked Soup did Jim come by. He said, "Yeah. But he seemed a little distant in his conversation. Not like he usual self. You know Miss Val at one time I couldn't make that boy shout his month.

Today I couldn't get two words out of his mouth. He's upstairs with Miss Charmaine. Dinner's ready in about an hour. I didn't want to disturb them." "I'll let them know. Jim's been through a lot these last few weeks. We have to bear with them for a while.

There may be some hard times ahead for the both of them and we all need to be there for them." "I understand Miss Val. CSM asked me to do a dinner setup for the COC. They're going to be working late over there tonight."

I went up to the room to change for dinner and to tell Charmaine dinner was almost ready. When I walked in her room she was wiping her face. I asked her what is wrong. You feel alright? She said, "I'm fine Miss Val. I'll be down shortly." "Where's Jim." "He went over to the COC. They had an 'After Action Review' to finish. He left about twenty minutes ago." "I'm sorry I missed him. So how is he?"

"He's going to be fine. He's been through a lot, but he going to be fine. He's home now with family and people who loves him. The twins are due in a few weeks and we'll have our hands full to keep us busy.

I'm looking forward to that." "Well, that wonderful. I guess I'll see him tomorrow. You're staying here for a while?" "We haven't discussed that yet." "Well, I hope so.

It may be best with everything that's still going on. It's whatever you and Jim decide. You are more than welcome to stay. I truly do enjoy your company. Dinner should be ready shortly," as I walked out the room.

After dinner Jai and I went over to the COC to get some insight on what the next few days is going to be like. Chief, Daniel and the rest of the team's participates were going over the plan.

As we walked in Daniel and Jim was at words about who was on lead with the mission and who was covering the COC. Jim was saying, "CSM, this is my lead, and Stephanie is my daughter. Just like when DJ was in trouble. You did not want anyone to do that mission but you, because of how personal this was to you.

Dammit CSM, god dammit this is how I feel about this mission. I need to go. I need to feel I am doing something to find my daughter." "Dammit Jim, you are not going. I am not going to put you through this. You are still injured. You are not ready to do this. I will not let you do this."

"CSM, I've got to do this. I've got to do this for her. I owe her that much. I was never there for her or her mother. They are both depending on me. I will not let anyone stop me CSM not even you."

"OK! Jim-bob, stand-down and you too Dan. I've heard enough. Let's take this off line." They went out to the airfield. I looked at Jai and Tom, "What brought that on?" I asked. Tom offered "Well, you heard most of it. Why don't we take a break?"

I went out in the dining area and Jai and Eloise came over and sat. "Well, you know what's going to come of all that. Chief will put in all in perspective. He's very good at things like that," Jai reminded.

"Jim is going through a lot. He has a lot of guilt he's going through. Also considering what he just went through in LA. He has a lot on his mind. He doesn't want any pity.

He just needs to gain his own self dignity. We all know the person Jim is. We must respect him during these times. We all owe him that much. I know I do."

I stood and walked out to the wall and thought, *Jim is like a son to me, and I pray father you give him strength to get through this,* as tears formed in my eyes. *Father he is so confused and in so much pain. Help him Lord, help him Lord please.* Chief walked back in. I asked, "Everything straight?" "I hope, they're two of a kind," he replied as he shook his head. "Let's get back to that meeting."

They finished the meeting without any other disturbance. Jim and Daniel didn't return until the meeting was over. Jai and I were to return to the COC in the morning along with Jim. I thought to myself, this is going to be a very interesting mission.

I was asleep when Daniel got home. He woke me up as he sat on the bed. I asked "Is everything alright between you and Jim?" He said, "We got an understanding. That about how it ended." "What lead to that big disturbance?" He took a deep breath" "Jim wants to take the lead on the mission. I don't feel he's mentally as well as physically able to handle the mission. I can see his point but just as chief tried to explain it to Jim he has too many issues going on in his life at this time.

We cannot afford to put any more pressure on him in the field. He's like a walking time bomb. This is one of the most if not the most sensitive mission we have ever endured. I know he wants to be there if and when we do find Stephanie. We cannot have a person on this mission who may crack under the circumstances or what the situation may incur.

I tried to make him understand but, he is so wrapped up in his own self-pity and his desire and need to make things right. He can and would be more of a problem for the rest of us on the team. He's mad and he's hurting because those people have hurt him in more ways than one. He's afraid he's going to be too late to save her.

He's afraid he's going to disappoint Stephanie's mom who has put her last bit of trust in the man who she feel is her last result.

See Val, before chief left us on the airfield and went back to the COC he told us this is something Jim and I needed to work out before we leave tomorrow. The last thing he said as he walked off he does not want us to break up a lifetime relationship we've have because of our hard heads. He said he wants this ended by the time we get back to the COC and that is a direct order.

I said we got you chief, Jim didn't say anything. Chief held out his hand for Jim to shake and said come on Jim-bob man we three been through too much together.

We're the best of the best at what we do and we need each other more this time then we have ever. We just have to know when to tell the other when he needs to stand down. Jim-bob son, this is that time you need to stand down and let us take the lead on this mission. We don't and we can't afford to lose you.

I told him when we couldn't locate you in LA; that was the most stressful time for the two of us. We thought we had lost you. Dan kept saying no man we'll find him. I can feel he's here somewhere and I'm going to find my boy if I have to tear every one of these god forsaken building down in this rat infested hole of a place. I kept saying chief he's down here somewhere I know it and I can feel it.

Chief told him, When Dan called me the day he got word on your location. I could hear it in his voice. He was overwhelmed. To be honest with you, I thought the worse.

Dan kept saying he's down in your area you got to go get him. No matter what the situation is don't leave him down there. I'm on my way. That's when we got there and met up down in the hotel. We did not want to face your situation alone.

We went up to the room, they said you were in, and that's where we found you. The paramedics were there and you were lying there in that tub of melting bloody ice. Dan asked were you alive and the paramedics said yes except he's minus his left kidney. He said he'll be alright once we get him to the hospital.

The ice is what kept him alive. Most bleed out in his situation. That's when we both fell apart. I went to the hospital and Dan stayed to wrap up some things. At the hospital is when we decided this was a mission we were determined to finish. We owe that to you Jimbo and to your family.

You been there for us through all the assignment and mission we had to endure. You have been there for us and been our back up and third man on the triangle. It is our job now to take care and protect you and your family. We need you here to call the shots in the COC.

No one knows this job better than you and Eloise. You are our eyes, ears and shot caller we can't do this without you being here. Jimbo let us do this one for you. You're always there for us. We need and want to do this for you."

Daniel concluded and said, "After that the tone in our conversation was much better. Chief and Jimbo shook hands and gave each a hug. We did a fist dapped and chief walked back to the meeting.

Jim and I talked for a while and we came to the conclusion he may be suffering from PTSD. I told him I wanted him to make an appointment at the VA and he said he would. So that pretty much where we left it. He's going to spend the night here with Charmaine." I then said, "I'm glad he agreed to that." We then went to sleep.

We all met down for breakfast at the usual time. Charmaine wasn't feeling very well so Jim took her breakfast to her room. Daniel and chief left later that evening for Rio de Janeiro.

Jai, I and the rest of the team started our day at the COC. Jim arrived early before we got in. Daniel had called the COC earlier and informed us that an auction was taking place in Rio in a few days and they were going to be there.

Tom gave us our morning update informing us that he believed this is going to be the most difficult missions we have ever been involved in. Daniel and Chief have left for Rio and they will meet up with their contacts that have been having eyes on the ground since they left Los Angeles.

They have been placed within the city as foreign businessmen and will be bidding on the various items they will be auctioning in the next few days.

I must warn you from what we have observed through the feed, we have found some very difficult things that are taking place in that area." "Like what?" I asked.

"They use children to beg, steal and kill for them." I asked, "What you mean children?" He continued, "Val, children they have kidnapped or stolen from various countries around the world. Some volunteered believing they are helping their families back home in their country. They are beaten, starved and raped for the enjoyment of the men and women who is in control of them.

If they try to escape they are sometimes killed and thrown away like trash or garbage for shark bait. They make it known to these children what the outcome would be if they try to escape. The worse thing about this is they are being controlled by other children in the group.

Their ages ranges from seven to twelve years. The younger ones are sold to black market orphanages where they may end up in some foreign country, most of the time they end up here in the United States. Most of the places that buy those young babies don't do it for the money, what they're trying to do is save their little lives.

The other thing some of those babies belongs to those girls who has been captured. They are placed in a baby mill." He hesitated and said, "Don't say I didn't warn you. It going to get worse. Let's take a break."

I went over to where Jim was sitting. I ask him how was he doing, He said he was doing fine, but chief them thinks I have PTSD. "That's why they wouldn't let me go with them to find my daughter."

I said, "I need to take a walk after that bit of information," "You mind some company." "No not at all. So, how you feel about that?" I asked. "I don't think I have PTSD but, chief and CSM wants me to make an appointment at VA." "So, are you going to?" "Chief pretty much said that's what he wants me to do. I guess it's what I need to do if I want to keep my job."

"I don't think it has anything to do with your job, most likely it's about how much they care about you. You have been through a very traumatic experience. They both thought they had lost you.

You are just like the both of them. Daniel was just like you when he first lost his son DJ. He suffered through the lost for many years. Mainly because he was there in country and through no fault of his own he felt it was his fault. You know what he went through you and chief was there.

Knowing the person Daniel is. He is very concerned about your state of mind." "Miss Val, I'm not losing it. I may be a little stressed, but I can handle it." "Yeah, that's what we all said until something happens causing us to fall apart.

That's what happened to Daniel and that's what happened to me. All it takes is one thing or memory that sparks the situation and you could be like a stick of dynamite totally out of control. You'll have, if you haven't already had, flash backs to those traumatic moments and you'll began to react to them.

The thing you must find within yourself is a means of calmness and stability. You'll have to be able to talk about it. You will need to be able to talk about it without getting mad or letting it upset you.

This is why chief and CSM wants you to see VA. They can help you. They helped me when I came home. They can help you to get through this. Even though it's not military related, you are a veteran and you are entitle to those benefits."

"Daniel told me that you helped him see he was suffering from PTSD." "I didn't really help him, I only listen to him. I just let him talked it out. It was something he really needed to do. I didn't force it out of him.

I just let him start talking about it on his own. Like I said, I just listened. He did the same for me when Q-Tip got killed. For a long time I could not even say the word kill, when it came to Q-tip's demised. One day I was in my room and Daniel came in and I just fell apart. He had to tell me I was suffering from PTSD. I finally realized it.

One thing you must realize when it comes to PTSD you must talk it out. You don't have to join no group because I found so often you can get caught up in the group's feeling. I start realizing that when I came back from Saudi.

I met a lady who was not a doctor nor a psychologist, but a person who had been working with soldiers returning from the war and was having problem trying to readjust back into society from being or seeing some horrendous acts or things that had occurred on deployment.

She told us at one of our so called group meetings. PTSD is not a disease that you catch, but a condition. It's a condition that's the results of some horrendous act that took place in their life. It's when you do not know what to do to clear those thoughts out your mind. Your reaction is usually negative or hostile.

One of the main things you need to do is think it out. Not think it out to be vengeful. Talk it out of what happened. Tell your story so you can slowly try to put the pieces back together in your life. Your life is like a puzzle. I'm not going to go into detail explaining the thing about the puzzle. Each piece of your puzzle represents a piece of your life that is in disarrangement.

You have a responsibility to yourself to somehow manage to put it back together. It's going to take time. This is not something that will magically fall in place. You're the one that has to put it all together.

No one can do that for you. No medication can really do that for you, not even therapy. You have to be your own therapist. It is up to you to find which pieces goes where.

You have to find out whom or who plays the role of each piece. You have to identify how important each of the people are in your life and where they fit into your life. Keep in mind each of these individuals are pieces of the puzzle you are trying to put back together.

So, to be honest with you the best place to start is at the VA. There are good people there who cares a lot about veterans who are suffering from PTSD or who are suffering from some traumatic experience as yours.

You have to also remember when Stephanie comes back, when we get her back, she's probably going to go through the same thing you're going through. This whole ordeal is going to be a traumatic experience for her. She's going to need someone to talk to who has been through or is going through what she has gone through.

Being kidnapped and used as a pawn for whatever means her captive has deemed her for. She's going to need you to help get her through this. Her mother doesn't know this stuff. But you do. You are an expert at what you do.

You have seen everything this type of life these people can throw at you. You are or can be an example for her as a person who has survived the hands of these notorious criminal minded animals.

So, you have to get yourself together for Stephanie. Stephanie is a young lady in the prime of her life as a college student. Kidnapped and stolen with no thought of anything like this ever happening to her.

Her whole world being snatched from her by someone she took as a friend. Jim I can only imagine how you feel and what's going through your mind, but you got to be ready to help her when she gets home.

She's going to have a whole lot of issues that nobody is going to be able to handle. But, you have an idea of what it's all about considering what you went through in Los Angeles. So, if anybody has any idea how to help Stephanie is going to be you. It's going to be your opportunity to be the father you did not know you were.

The worse part about this is Stephanie is going to go through hell trying to come back and pick up her life. Her life has almost been totally destroyed. But she's got one great thing going for her, and that is her father being the type of person you are; and I know you are and will be there for her. So, you my dear friend is just gonna have to get your stuff together in order to help her.

I know you want to be there but, you can't be there if you haven't got yourself together. You have to be ready when we get her back home. You have to be ready to handle what she's gonna go through. She's gonna go through a hell of a lot. Look at yourself now. Look at yourself now mentally and physically. She's going to go through much more than what you have gone through.

Stephanie has been gone almost eight months now and we don't even know if we're going to find her. And when we do find her we don't know what kind of condition she's going to be in. We can only imagine the worse kind of condition she's going to be in considering who her captives are.

You are the only person that would only be prepared to help her. We cannot throw her in a hospital, and hope for the best; but we will do everything we can to help her.

You know you owe this to yourself as well as to Stephanie. So you better get your stuff right, because once we get her home it not going to be a matter of let her get herself together, let her rest. You have got to get her back focus on what is going on in life. I sure hope and pray that you will be ready for this.

It not something that we can just hope works out right. It's something that we needs to help her and you are the main person that going to be able to help Stephanie.

By God's grace, you came out of it alive; and it is wrong that you went through, what you went through. But, you got to understand in God's eyes everything happens for a reason; and he never gives us more than we can handle.

So keep in mind by you getting well is more to Stephanie's advantage than it is to yours. Although you got the twins coming, you still got to understand Stephanie is going to need you a whole lot. Y'all got a lot of catching up to do and a lot of repairing to do. So keep in mind this is not all about you, but, right now it is about you.

It's about Stephanie also. Be ready to tell her your story when need too. You kept saying you were not there for her. Take advantage of that opportunity and be ready when she comes home. I know you will do the right thing. You always have. Changing the subject, I said, "I think it's time we headed back to the COC." He agreed. We headed back to the hangar to the COC.

When we got back to the COC, Tom informed us we have some update on the mission. Daniel and Chief had landed in Rio and they will be meeting with their counter parts later that evening. I asked, "Do we have any idea what their plan is?" He said, "No not at his time.

They were going to scout around and try to get a feel of things. Dan and chief did mention they have three other teams they are working with. A John Woo, retired intelligence Colonel.

He's a part of the Polaris teams out in the field. He volunteered to support Dan and his team in country. Chief and Daniel are going to do some recon before they all meet up."

"Well, do they have a plan or are they going to play it by ear," I asked. "Val, at this point we have no idea. You have to realize this and Jim can vouch on this. Daniel and Chief are very good at adlibbing. They have a tendency to make it up as they go along.

I've heard very good stuff about COL Woo. He and Chief pulled off some tough assignment back in Afghanistan. Most of his team has done this kind of stuff before but not against this group. Like I said he volunteered his support." Jim added, "We were going to use him and his people once before but it worked out without them. I've never met him but Chief speaks highly of him. If Chief says he's good, then who am I, to say anything different."

Tom concluded, "This is pretty much all we got for now. I suggest we call it a night and pick it up in the morning. Let's say about 06:00. If something happens during the night, you know the drill."

Eloise dropped me off back at the mansion, Jim and Jai had some things they had to finish up. Eloise commented, "I assume you and Jim had a very good conversation out on the runway."

"I just told him a few things I thought he should know. He's going through a lot and he does know exactly how to handle it or what he should do. So, I just told him what I thought and why I think it's something he may need to do.

Eloise, he's really lost in trying to figure out what he needs to do. A lot has been dropped on him, a daughter he knew nothing about, a wife who is about to give birth to a set of twins and his own personal problem pertaining to his own situation.

Jim really needs our support and I'm afraid his going to break if we are not going to be there for him. We need to be there for him more so now than ever.

I think of all the times he's been there for me, Daniel and this whole family. He's always been there and had our back. It's our time to be there for him. I'm just really worried about him."

"Val, I'm just glad you had that talk with him. I'm not very good at giving heart to heart talks about things like this. It hurt me knowing he is going through this. He is strong but he can be vulnerable at times. He thinks so highly of you. You are the only one that can speak to him in a motherly manner and encourage him to make the right decision.

Neither Tom nor I could do that because we all work too close. But you Val, you have that nurturing instinct that is always there when needed. Just like Chief said, you are the mother hen in this family or "hen house" as he calls it even though CSM thinks he's the "Rooster in this Chicken Coop".

Well, that's all I got to say about that. I'm so glad you and CSM got married. You both make this family feel like what a family should be." "I better go in and check on Charmaine" Eloise gave me a hug and said give her my love.

I went in and checked on Charmaine in her room. She informed me Jim had called and said he had a long talk with you. She then said he confessed it was more you talking than him.

He had been really thinking about some of the things you had mentioned and he has some things he needs to do. So when he gets home we're going to discuss it." I said, "That's wonderful.

I just want you to know I am not trying to tell him what to do; and I know what Daniel and I both went through and we were there for each other when we went through our times of PTSD. I still haven't totally gotten over mine's and I still have some setbacks and I have noticed at time Daniel does too.

But we don't let it takeover. How we handle it is the most important thing; and knowing you have family and loves ones to support you is the most important thing. I know you and Jim and the twins are going to be alright just let him know and show your support. I'm going to let you three get some rest, good night."

I went down to check on the crew Jai was setting in the kitchen talking to Soup. I told them I just came down to check on the crew before I turn-in for the night. I asked had anything happen since we left? She said, "No not really but Tom has team East extraction team and Col Woo team on alert. Tom said he didn't think anything was going to happen right away but just in case he wanted to be ready. Other than that it's pretty quiet over there Jim and Tom still there."

Jai then continued, "Speaking of Tom, What's this about Diane is supposed to get Janelle's house." "Oh, she tried but, nothing came of that. I'll tell you about that tomorrow. I'm going to bed. I see you two in the morning Good night. Oh, Soup did Jai tell you about our early breakfast at the COC." "Got you Miss Val, see you in the morning."

Jai and I left early for the COC. Soup had arrived just before we did with the morning chow. Tom said, "Grab your chow and come on in. We have a lot to cover this morning. We're running about four hours behind what's been happening. I need to warn you what you are about to witness may not be something you ladies may feel comfortable watching.

I myself felt somewhat very uncomfortable watching this feed. Before I show you any of this footage I will give you a somewhat scenario of Chief's and Daniel's role in what they are doing. Neither one is on the footage but you can hear their voice in the background.

Col Woo is their go between. He is doing their bidding for them. Chief and Daniel are located in two different areas and Woo is bidding for each of them. They are bidding on the individuals by picture and according to their performance.

I must warn you some of the pictures are of very young individuals. They're from the ages of five to twenty five, both males and female from various nationality and countries.

If you find what you see is too hideous to watch, I encourage that you remove yourself from this immediately. I repeat these footages are not something you would want to ever see again. I know I don't." I ask Tom, "Just what Chief and Daniel trying to do or should I say attempting to achieve."

"Well, after y'all left last night Daniel and Chief met up with their counter-part, Col Woo. He gave them the rundown on how the bidding was taking place. The so call auctioneer is nowhere to be seen or found. He is located or may be in some other country.

Each bid is handled by remote control by pressing a number which represents the individual bidder. Once the bid is closed the individual is immediate sent to the winning bidder.

They will receive their merchandise within 48 hours of receipt of their funds. All transactions are done in cash which means no traceable evidence." "Well," I asked, "How are they going to catch these people?"

"Val, you may not like what I am about to say but, they are not there to catch anyone doing these horrendous acts. They are there to get Stephanie and whoever else they can help out of this mess. I know you are not going to like what I just said but that is Chief's and Dan mission and they are going to stick to that.

Let me also say these people have been doing this for a very long time. There are countries and leaders high on the ladder that is a part of this kind of crime.

Although this is a crime on our children and humanity one or two people cannot be the one to bring an end to it. It's people like Col Woo who's fighting every day to bring an end to these types of heinous crimes.

So, Val we can only do a little at a time to try to bring an end to these kinds of things. So, being that I have told you what I have been directed by both my bosses, I will roll the footage. As I mentioned and suggested at any time, any of you who desire to leave for you to do so."

I was so tempted to get up and leave, but I sat there and watch some of the footage. I got sick to my stomach and tears started to slow rolled down my face. I got up and walk out of the building and started walking down the airstrip. I just couldn't take anymore. Jai must had followed me out and called to me.

I stopped and let her catch up to me. I started to ball as if every one of the children I saw was children I knew. It was one of the most painful things I have ever seen in my life." I kept saying Jai, "How could they do that to those poor babies.

My heart hurts just seeing them being forced upon like they were nothing but animals. They all should burn in hell for eternity every last one of them. Someone got to do something." "Val, I don't know what to say but, you left a little too soon.

Stephanie's picture came up next, but they cut the feed." "What you mean her picture came up next? Did Jim see her?" "That's how we knew it was her" "Val, Jim fell apart when he saw her and the screen went black." "Oh, my God this could kill him." "Well, at least he didn't see anything else" "Jai, he's vulnerable this could push him over the edge. I need to go back in there."

When I got back in the building I asked what happen. Tom said, "Someone must had cut the feed I think it was Dan." I asked, "How you know?" "Val, this is a late feed from four hours ago. Only Dan or Chief could have done it.

They wouldn't want Jim see what was on that feed. So one of them must have done it." "So when is our next scheduled communication?" "In about an hour we should know something then." I went over and talked to Jim.

He was drinking some coffee. "Miss Val, I saw her. It was only a glimpse of her but it was her." "So, what you think?" "I don't know, all I do know is if I saw her, Chief and CSM saw her too. I know they're going to get her." I thought to myself, *"that–a–boy, keep thinking those positive thoughts."*

The call came in two hours later, Tom said they got her, it's a deal. They should see her later tonight. Val, Dan said they got some things they need to tie up and they'll see us in a couple of days.

I turned to Jim and said, "See Jim you were right, they got her." He then got up, took his ear piece out his ear and walked out the room. I started to get up and follow him. Eloise grabbed my arm and said, "Val, let him go."

Tom then informed me Dan said he'll call you later. I said thanks. Jim came in and said he'll take the watch. I asked him was he ok? He said, "Yes Miss Val. I just need to do my part now." I gave him a hug and told him, "I see him later."

Eloise and I left and headed back to the mansion. Jai stayed back to give some last minute instruction to her teams' leaders. When we arrived back at the house we got the word all teams were airborne and enroute with the package except Chief, CSM and COL Woo. They should be back in a day or so. Tom said Dan would call me when he gets the chance on his office line at home.

Daniel called about midnight on my cell and told me to go to the office and he'll call me right back. As I walked in his office the phone rang. I clicked on the monitor and Daniel came on the screen. He apologized for not returning with the other team members.

He then informed me he has another mission to assist COL Woo and his team. I asked was it dangerous. He said, "It's pretty much what they just did but it has to do with trying to extract some kids out of an area in which I can't reveal to you at this moment.

You'll have to handle things back there concerning Jim and Stephanie. I won't be there when they get home. They'll be flying into El Paso airfield. I need you and Eloise to take the lead on this. I'm not sure how Jim is going to handle all this. Also I made arrangement for Jai team to pick Stephanie's mother up and bring her down there." "Where she's going to stay?" "I'm not sure but Chief got Eloise working that."

"OK Daniel. I just hope this doesn't turn out to be one of those Cluster bombs." "Well, I don't think it will but you and Eloise usually know how to handle those kinds of problems." "I know there won't be a problem with Charmaine, but I don't know Stephanie or her mother. Plus I don't know what frame of mind Stephanie is in or her mom.

Now how long you two are going to be gone." "It should take a couple of days and we should be home soon." "I hope you two get home before all hell does break loose." "Come on, Val I have yet to see a situation that you or Eloise can't handle. Plus I asked Jai to stick around just in case things get out of hand."

"Thanks a lot. Three women trying to handle a somewhat irate young female who has just been set free from being abducted."

"Val, I have the greatest confidence in you and your two comrades in helping to handle this situation." "We'll see. You know you going to owe me big on this."

"Whatever you want, it's yours. We'll discuss that when we get back." "Just keep in mind we have a wedding to prepare for as well as the annual holiday gala to prepare for." "I know. I'll be back in time. Well, I'll see you in a couple of days. I love you." "I love you too" and we both hung up.

Eloise called me the next day and said, "I understand you got your marching orders from CSM." "Yeah! You'd think he's still running the company."

She then said, "Val, I'll be perfectly honest with you Daniel still runs the company to a point. Chief is only there to put out the fires as he always did in the past."

"So, what Chief has to say about that?" "He doesn't care. It's pretty much the way it was before his so called retirement. Chief gives the clan advice and Daniel most of the times goes along with it. That's why he made Chief the CEO.

They have always been partners and they made Jim and DJ both executive partners. You and I sets somewhere in that chain also without a vote. We're just automatic volunteered by our husbands to do various things.

Why, do you think they're always putting us down in that COC when something always comes up? I asked chief one day in the office why they always pick us to do the special missions at the COC. He said because we can always depend on you doing the right thing.

I told him that's not a good answer. He said well my dear that all you going to get because it's the truth. So Val now you know why we're always on detail at the COC."

"Well, when are they supposed to land at El Paso airport?" "In a couple of hours about noon we are supposed to meet Stephanie's mother there also. She's arriving at about eleven o'clock. I'm picking you up in about fifteen minutes." "Thanks for the heads up. I'll meet you out front."

When we arrived at the airport Anna waved us down from the curve at the arrival area. We had no idea what she looked like. I asked Eloise, "Is that her?" "Don't ask me I have no idea what she look like."

"Oh, this is great, here we are picking someone up and we don't know what they look like." As we pulled up to the curve she walked over to the SUV and asked were we Val and Eloise. We both said yes. She said, "Jim told me to look for the SUV with HIE, LLC Triangle logo on the door."

I got out and introduced myself as Eloise stayed in the SUV. We helped her get her baggage and tried to make her feel welcome. We told her we had to go over to the other side of the airport where the private jets came in because Stephanie was coming in on one of the company's jets and it should be landing in about forty-five minutes.

She was very anxious and somewhat quiet. I tried to make her feel at ease by telling her Jim and both our husbands were among the ones who rescued her daughter.

I told her we have not seen her but Eloise's and my husband both had. She asked were they the ones bringing her back. We told her no but one of the other team members was. She asked, "So what do y'all company do?" Jim wouldn't tell her. He just said we got Stephanie and she's on her way home. That's when she started to cry. I told her Jim has a lot on his plate right now, but we'll try to explain all this to you and Stephanie once we get you two united.

The jet pulled into the hangar with HIE, East on it. It was one of Jai's extraction team that brought her home. I looked at Anna and said "She should be getting off in any minute now."

JT one of the team's pilot wave as they pulled in. We got out the SUV and waited while they open the door and they lowered the steps to the plane.

Anna couldn't hold herself from the excitement. She ran to the plane as Stephanie stepped out the door. Stephanie a somewhat beautiful light-skin young lady considering what she has been through.

Tears began to fill my eyes and Eloise as we stood and the mother and daughter both fell to their knees as they hugged each other. We couldn't do anything but relish the moment as we stood and hugged each other.

JT walked over and said, "Miss Val, we are honored to be able to deliver this very delicate package back home." I gave JT a hug and thanked him. "If you ladies excuse me I have to report in to the COC and my boss." I said, "Don't let us stop you." We then went over to introduce our selves to Stephanie.

She came over still holding her mom's hand and said, "You must be Miss Val, the man they called the CSM wife and you must be Miss Eloise the man they called Chief's wife." She then gave us both a big hug and said you don't know how grateful I am for your husbands bringing me home.

I still can't believe this nightmare is over with. It's been so long. I can't believe I'm back in my own country with my mother and good people.

I then interrupted and said, "We have to get you over to our command center and get you debrief and then get you both settled in." She didn't have any bags and Anna had only one. We all climbed in to the SUV and headed back to the COC.

When we arrive at the COC everyone was busy working some crises that had just occurred. Tom said, "CSM and Chief is in route home they should be arriving some time tomorrow or earlier if Chief can get a good tail wind."

Jim was sitting with his back turn talking with someone through his earpiece. He took his earpiece out and got up and stared at his daughter for the first time in the flesh. I could see he was crying for the first time.

Anna spoke up and said, "Stephanie, I like you to meet James E. Harris, your father." I then said, "He is the third side that makes up the Triangle on the symbol for HIE, LLC. He is the spearhead that keeps this Corporation going. Jim as we call him is who keeps my husband CSM and Chief on point when they are on missions.

She ran over and gave him a big hug and didn't want to let him go. She said, "I thought you were dead." He looked down at her and said, "No. I didn't know about you until a few months ago and your mother showed up at my door needing my help."

Anna said, "I didn't have anyone else to turn to. You had been gone almost two months and the police and the school security was no help. So I thought Jim was still in the Army and maybe he could help but he wasn't.

So he eventually got his very good friends involved and after several months trying to locate where you are or where it lead to all this." As she looked around in amazement and asked, "What do y'all do?"

Jim then said, "We're a very hi-tech corporation that works for the federal government from time to time. That's about all I can tell you." Anna then said, "I don't care what type of work you do. All I know is you brought my baby home and I thank you all so very much."

I then asked Eloise have we got a place for them to stay. She said, "Yes, they going to be staying with Chief and me. That way we can all be together and I can get them over here to debrief in the morning. I'm pretty sure they are ready to just relax and get reacquainted. So, whenever you are ready I'll take you over and get y'all settled in."

I then had Jai, who's been quiet through all that was going on in the Center drop me off at the mansion. As we got in the SUV she said, "Never a boring day at the Howards. I love visiting y'all.

To think I'm going to be here for the next few months." I then asked, "So what's so important that Daniel and Chief had to stay back and finish up some unfinished business?"

"Why you asking me, you know they don't always tell me what they're up to." "Jai it don't matter, but I know they are using your team as the extraction team for whatever they are doing before coming home.

So, you know what's going on." "Well, you don't have to twist my arm, but Chief said they need someone on hand that has knowledge of prenatal care." "When are they expected back?" "Early tomorrow morning." "Daniel told me he'll fill me in when he gets back.

I believe it has something to do with Stephanie." As we walked in the house the crew came running to the door. Soup said, "CSM called just before you walked in said he needed to talk to you before he got here in the morning. He'll call you back in about an hour. I mumble as I walked up the stairs, "Now what done happened." I came back down and waited for Daniel's call.

Jim walked in and stopped me before I walked in his office. I asked him how things were going. He said, "Pretty much the same. I'm not sure how to handle the fact that I am a father with a grown daughter." I told him to come on in the office while I waited for CSM's call.

He came in and sat in the chair across from CSM's desk. He then said, "Miss Val, what am I supposed to say to my daughter. I don't know her and she doesn't know me. What are we supposed to talk about?

I don't want to bring up anything that makes her remember or think about all what she just went through." "Well, you're going to have to talk about it sooner or later. I don't know what to tell you. Just don't let what you went through hold you back from what you may have to do. From what I've observed, Stephanie looks much stronger than we think she is."

"I don't know Miss Val I don't know what to do next. It's like being in the eye of the hurricane and not knowing what to do. Should I wait it out and see what happens or should I take a chance and it's the wrong thing to do." "Jim I don't know what to tell you. This has got to be one of those times you have to figure on your own. No matter what I or anyone tell you.

That's why Eloise and Chief had decided that it would be best that Stephanie and Anna stay at their place than anywhere else. Eloise and Chief has worked and been around you more than anyone and they can pretty much answer any question they might have when it came to the COC or what we do as a company." "Miss Val, I'm just afraid she will hate me after all these years and suddenly here I am, her long lost father.

She never knew anything about me and for that matter I never knew anything about her until a few months ago. How am I supposed to react to this type of situation? I don't want to blame her mother."

"Then don't, what are you blaming her for. Not telling you, that you have a daughter long time ago. Does that change anything, not really? This type of situation happens all the time. We're just fortunate we have the resources to do what we had to do to get her back." The phone began to ring.

"That must be CSM, I need to go and check on Charmaine and the twins. Good night Miss Val." I picked up the phone. "Hey babe." "Hey, yourself how things going? Everything's fine. It's quiet now."

"There's more to this situation than we thought. We found out when Stephanie was abducted she was three months pregnant. Evidently when they found that out they put her in the baby mill.

She had the baby about three months ago. Once she had the baby they sold the baby on the black market." "On the black market, oh my God!" "Well, to make a long story short. We had to go to Malaysia to get the baby from one of the orphanages that handle abducted babies.

Being that the baby is bi-racial if he was not adopted or sold he would be raised and then used as many of the young boys are in these situations. He would be taught and forced to steal, rob and kill if he has too. This is the life of many of these young boys has in order to eat and live.

We do not know how he ended up there but COL Woo found him through his contact. Since the baby is bi-racial, as his mother, he is not wanted by most of those wanting a child and they prefer girls rather than boys.

He didn't have a name so we call him "little Jim". Chief is spoiling him as we speak." "How did you know who he was?" "Woo has an inside contact at the orphanage who contacted him, a bi-racial baby was dropped off there a month ago.

He contacted us when he got word and said he heard a bi-racial girl gave birth to a bi-racial baby boy and they fear his life may be in danger because of his race."

"So, what are you going to do now?" "We're going to bring little Jim home to his mother. Babe, I need you to get in touch with Danielle to meet us at the clinic when we get in.

We should be there in about four hours. I'm going to have to cut the feed now. We're about to enter in a radio silence area. The screen went dark as he hung up."

I went out to the kitchen where Jai and Soup was and told them what Daniel had just told me. I then went up to my room and soaked in the tub before going to bed. My thought went back to Q-Tip as I laid my head down. His presence was still in the room. I thought maybe it's time we got that place in Norfolk as a summer place, as I dozed off to sleep.

CHAPTER Nine

I awoke to the smell of bacon and SOS in the kitchen. I thought to myself Daniel must be home. I got up and went down stairs. I could hear voices coming from the kitchen, but none sounded like Daniel's voice. "Morning Miss Val, everyone's over at the COC this morning.

You want to eat here? I can fix you a plate." "Did Daniel them come in this morning?" "Yes, Miss Val. They went straight to Miss Danielle's clinic and then they're going to the COC. CSM came in but he didn't want to wake you." "Did they have the baby with them?"

"I didn't see a baby but CSM was alone. He came in showered and changed clothes and then left. I'm headed that way with morning chow, and can I offer you a lift?" "Thanks Soup, give me a chance to throw something on." "I'll finish loading the meals if you need me." "That's fine Soup I'll meet you out back."

When we arrived at the COC everyone was there. Daniel, Chief were talking with Tom. Daniel came over and gave me a kiss and said "I missed you, babe." "I missed you too, so what's going on?"

"Well, if you feel like taking a walk I'll try to fill you in before everyone else get in." We walked out towards the airfield. "Well, Stephanie doesn't want little Jim." "What you mean she doesn't want little Jim?" "Chief said, when he got in this morning with the baby, Stephanie said she didn't want the baby, she had put him up for adoption." "Why, Daniel? Did her mom know this or even knew she was pregnant for that matter?" "We don't know.

These are questions we've been asking ourselves. When chief got in this morning he said she didn't want to talk about it. She wanted to put it all behind her now that she'd back home." "Daniel I don't understand, does Jim know this?" "That's the thing Val. Jim doesn't know any of this.

Charmaine has an appointment this morning and Jim is coming after the appointment. We didn't want to mention any of this until after he gets in. As if he doesn't have enough on his mind. We didn't want him to have this on his mind also." "But Daniel, he has to know."

"Well, Eloise is on her way in with them. We'll see what happen. I just wanted to give you heads up before everyone gets in. Val, I really need your help and support on this."

"Daniel, honey I hear you but what is it that you want from me?" "Well, I don't know maybe it's something that happened back at school. Whatever happened to her it happened before she got abducted.

Whether we know it or not Woo said it's probably what kept her alive or should I say saved her life. From what I've found out these are some vicious characters we were dealing with.

There are known governments that keep a closed eye to what is happening in their countries. Some are countries our government does business with." "Daniel, what are you looking to do or trying to do in reference to little Jim?"

"Val, I don't know but whatever it is, we're doing it for little Jim, as well as Stephanie's benefits." "Well, just keep in mind not every young woman who gives birth is ready or wants for motherhood. She may not be, because of the circumstances that lead to her pregnancy." "I know Val, this is something chief and I talked about in route back here, little Jim."

"What if we find out she got pregnant under some criminal mishap. What will you do with the baby than?" "I'm hoping it wasn't under that type of circumstances. It would lead to other issues that need to be resolved and how to handle it." "Well, you know isn't that where she met that so call friend that took her to the party up in Hollywood?"

"That's a possibility maybe I'll get some people on it. There has been known to some situations in the fraternities that are often kept quiet by the campus in some of those colleges.

That happened a lot when I was going to college in New Orleans. I'll have someone check into it when we get back." "Please, I just feel this may be her reason why." We started back to the command center.

When we got back, Eloise, Stephanie and her mom was in. Chief was holding little Jim. I could tell he had really gotten attached to that little guy. I could see the feeling was mutual. It was very interesting knowing the type of person Chief was.

Eloise came over to me and said, "Girl, we need to talk." "I know Daniel, just filled me in on what's been happening." We walked towards her office as she said, "Val, I don't think she wants that child." "Did she tell you that?" "No, but when she got word yesterday chief and CSM were bringing her son home. Her comment was I put him up for adoption.

They promised me they would find him a good home. I told her he's your son, it's not like he's a puppy or a dog for that matters. She said I'm too young to have a child. I'm still in college. I need to finish my education." "What did her mother say?" "She didn't say anything.

She told me later she had no idea Stephanie was pregnant before she got abducted. She thought her and her daughter had a very good relationship. They talked about everything. She thought they had no secret between them. I told her evidently you did."

"So what are they going to do?" "I don't know. Stephanie's still talking about adoption. Chief has really taken a liking to the little fellow. He's talking about becoming a foster parent. " "Is that at all possible?" "I don't know but it is a thought considering nothing is said about Anna taking the baby. I don't think she wants him either."

"I don't understand these are really serious situations that needs considering. It seems Stephanie is looking forward to going back to school. If she wants to but it's great for her to go back and finish her schooling.

My question is she ready for that or even going back to USC. Los Angeles is where her abduction took place. Well, I guess it's about time we go back and join the rest of the team.

Jim was in talking to Chief and CSM in Tom's office. Jai said they had been in the meeting for a while since Jim got there. She said they were discussing how they were going to handle getting Stephanie the proper counselling she needs. She was going to get debrief by Chief and CSM without the presence of her mother or father because this would interfere her being honest about any of the answers.

The group assemble for the after action review. Afterwards chief and CSM met to do their debriefing with Stephanie. The debriefing went on for about two hours.

The next day Jim met with Chaplain Anderson and Stephanie to discuss what they should do about their situation. He suggested they spend some time together to get to know each other. Chief and Eloise was made god-parents to Little Jim. They suggested Stephanie to stay with them while she goes through therapy. Stephanie enrolled in UT El Paso. Jim went to VA in El Paso for his PTSD.

Two weeks later Charmaine went into labor and gave birth to the twin at the mansion. They were two beautiful little babies. Danielle delivered them just as they were scheduled. They named them Kevin and Kristina.

The Thanksgiving holiday brought many guest to the mansion so Charmaine and Jim decided to move back into their house after the babies were born. This gave us time to prepare for the holiday and DJ's and Trinity's wedding.

DJ stayed at the mansion as we prepared for the holiday and the wedding. They had a church wedding at the chapel on Fort Bliss. Chaplain Anderson did the ceremony. Daniel was the best man. They were all in Army mess white uniforms and ceremonial sabers.

Trinity was a breathtakingly beautiful bride in a beautiful white gown with a short train and pumpkin orange colored roses for her bouquet. Her bride's maids were in strapless autumn orange floor length gowns.

The Christmas season was quickly approaching. Tom informed us Diane was moving back to Seattle to be near her immediate family. She was tired of being in a place where she was not wanted or needed. Since he had started working for Daniel he had changed and he was not the man she first married.

She was going to file for divorce. She felt his job was more important than their marriage. She will not be attending the ball. He didn't appear at all disappointed. I think we all were happy that she was not attending. We were all excited about having our Christmas celebration for the first time without any surprising interruptions.

"Soup's Kitchen Catering" did the catering for all the events. On our New Year's Eve anniversary party, Daniel presented me with a gift I always wanted a summer house on the beach in Norfolk, VA.

Since the holidays had drawn down. Thus, we had decided to spend some time in the mansion and enjoy our family. I decided to put more time into working on my novels.

My publisher had been on me about finishing my next two books. I decided it was time I finished them. I finally realize our life was the main essence of my books. I laid across the bed and closed my eyes and drifted off asleep. I heard a voice say, "Can I join you" as he laid beside me. I mumbled, "umm hum." He sat the clock and laid beside me and said "DJ got promoted to Master Sergeant. Trinity's pregnant."

"That's wonderful I'll call her tomorrow." "Our little family is growing" "It's not little anymore." "Sure you're right" as he kissed me on my forehead and said, "I love you so much." "I love you more" as I laid on his chest and listen to the peaceful sound of his heartbeat. We both dozed off asleep.

The End

FREE PREVIEW TO THE BOOK COVER LEAF SIDE PAGE FLAPS

He reached in the drawer of his writing table and checked the ammo in his weapon before he placed it in his "To go bag" and continued, "Val, I can't tell at this moment until chief read me on it. I have no idea how serious this is but, it is somewhat heavy stuff." "I figure that, you carrying your old standby, I haven't seen you pull that out since you were a contractor."

"I know honey, but I don't know what we're up against when we get to LA. I'll let you know, but I don't want you to tell Charmaine anything no matter how much pity you have for her not knowing. We must keep her calm and make sure you tell Soup that also. I'll make sure to pass that on to him on my way out." Daniel left later that evening,

The following evening Daniel called as he had promised. He informed me they were still chasing some leads that would probably end up as no luck. Chief has some leads that maybe some help on Jim's daughter's disappearance as well as his." "So you are saying Jim's disappearance and his daughter maybe somewhat linked." "No, Val, all I'm saying they may be tied in somehow together. All I can say Jim is alive. He has been seen but, where he is now is not known." "Well, that gives us some hope."

"At this moment, I know these could be some very treacherous and dangerous individuals." "Daniel, you are scaring me." "Honey, I don't mean to scare you but, I feel you need to know, that people dealing in human trafficking is dealing with more than just people. They deal in drugs, weapons and maybe even human organs. There is nothing they wouldn't stop at." "Daniel, you be very careful. I know how much you love Jim, and you would do anything to bring him home. Keep in mind you have a family to come home to also." "I will honey, and I love you too. I'll call you on the phone in my office from now on its more secured."

Soon to be Release

Forever My Love

Continuing Sagas

My Forbidden Love – A Soldier's Love Story
Love, Life's Eternal Promise
Love, Life's Eternal Flame
And
Love, Life's Endless Destiny